Seasons In Cancer

By

George S. J. Anderson

Hollis Books, LLC

VA   CA   NY

I wish to dedicate this book to all those
Who have had their lives affected by breast cancer.

A special dedication to:

Darlene and Terry
Sandy and Mike
Stacey and Joe

I would also like to dedicate this book
To everyone still fighting this disease
And especially
To those who have lost the battle,
But live on in our hearts…

Works previously published and included in this compilation are: The story, "Remember This," published independently in 1994, and the story , "Twelve Roses," published in "Silver Linings, The Other Side of Cancer," in 1997 as one of a collection of stories. Both stories were reedited for this collection, yet retain their original meaning and context. Two previously published poems included in this collection are: "Journeys," written in 1977, and published in "The World's Greatest Contemporary Poems," in 1981, and "The Hour of the Child," written in 1981, later published in "Our Twentieth Century's Greatest Poems," in 1982. "The Hour of the Child," was published again in 1998 as a single work in a collection of poems called, "Thoughts by Candlelight."

Cover art "Merlin (The Blue Dream) by George S. J. Anderson

Contents

Preface: (Beginnings)

After the nurse called her name, my wife decided to go into the back exam room by herself. After all, the bruising we were concerned about was already retreating into faded yellow patches beneath her arm and faint purples around the incision made by the surgeon two weeks ago. I was sitting in the waiting room for only a few minutes, aimlessly paging through an old magazine, when the surgeon appeared and asked me to come back to the exam room where my wife was waiting. I knew something was wrong when he said, "I'm afraid I have some bad news for you both."

I found my wife sitting in a chair beside the exam table with the examination gown still huddled over her shoulders. Despite the warm room, she was pale and shaking. I hunched down beside her and touched her arm. Her skin felt cold and my touch did nothing to affirm she even knew I was there. The surgeon looked gravely at us and quietly told me that my wife had breast cancer!

What went wrong? When did it all start? Was it caused by the accidental injury to her right breast only a few months before, or was it because she ate all the "wrong" foods? Did she work with "bad" chemicals now or at some other time in her life that made this happen? Didn't she get enough exercise? Did where we live have something to do with this? Did she get too much sun? Perhaps, not enough? Should she be taking vitamins? Which ones? If she had, would it have made any difference? Was this God's punishment on her? Did she do something wrong in her life to deserve this? Or, was it something I had done that brought this strange unholy justice on us both? How devastating would this lethal malignancy be on her? On us? On our son? What would happen to us all with this diagnosis of breast cancer?

It seems strange, almost impudent, to sit and write it all down, these many years later. When my wife was diagnosed with breast cancer, I felt as though our whole world had ended abruptly. In a sense, I was not wrong. The quiet realm we lived in, to that point in our lives, died on the day she was diagnosed with breast cancer. Camelot was burning. A terrible enemy had breached the walls. The essence of what we believed to be valuable changed as we grasped for that which our enemy, cancer, was trying to steal. Our lives of planning for next year and the years after it were gone. That certainty of waking up alive and in god health the next day was no longer a distinct or probable possibility. Our thoughts of watching our son grow up, graduating from high school and college, marrying, and seeing our grandchildren together became irrevocably changed with the words "breast cancer." Everything we believed as our future of possibilities disappeared, because cancer would not allow us any certainty of what "tomorrow" held. Sometimes it was difficult to consider "tomorrow" in terms of living through it, much less a span of time we could take for granted. After a cancer diagnosis crosses the threshold of one of the lives you care about, you start to savor the special moments of your life, and the lives around you, in an entirely different way.

Cancer invaded our home and lives like an unwelcome trespasser. It entered as quietly as a thief who came to steal something of profound value from the heart of our existence. Even if this thief were caught, the authorities would never be able to retrieve the sense of peace we felt before the violent intrusion into our personal sanctuary.

My wife's breast cancer affected me very deeply on many levels. After all initial treatments for the existing breast cancer were completed, we endured many long hours, days, weeks, and months waiting for the uncertain outcome. At times, after the treatments, I believed her life had been spared. Unfortunately, my uncertainty regarding the outcomes of her treatment could not be realized until several years had passed. Now with all the treatment options exhausted, we had to exist with the uneasy peace that cancer had invaded her life and forever robbed us of the security we once felt. It was still possible for cancer to reappear later in her life. Indeed, as her oncologist put it, "We will attempt to give her disease-free intervals of survival. It will not be a cure."

As a home robbed by thoughtless thieves, the repository of her life was violated by the presence of breast cancer. Never again would she sleep in complete serenity, unaware that cancer could be lurking in the dark recesses of her body. Never again could she sleep immersed in the quiet solitude of dreams because the thief of life might come again when she was not looking…when she was not prepared. As if she could ever prepare for such a thief…as if anyone could.

I remember those nights when I tried to stay awake after she received chemotherapy. I would watch her closely those first nights, observing the rise and fall of her chest, making sure each breath allowed her to survive the night. Sometimes her breathing seemed so shallow that I would put my ear close to her lips and simply listen and sense her expirations on my skin. Eventually, when I knew I had to fall into the abyss of sleep, I would reach out and hold her hand in that strange, surreal darkness. I needed to feel the warmth of her hand, just to feel that she was still alive. I had to resolve, in some way, a strange unreasonable fear that she had reacted to chemotherapy or succumbed to her cancer during the night. I didn't want her to die when I wasn't watching, or when I wasn't alert and clear enough to stop whatever might happen to her while she slept.

My fears of her dying were intense, as were the grinding changes that cancer and its treatment were to her. The whole ordeal seemed like some cruel absurd punishment for some forgotten unforgiving sin. I often wondered, in the old Biblical sense, what warranted this terrible atonement embodied by this cancer? What terrible injustice did she commit to deserve this? On the other hand, was I also being punished by this abomination of life? Would its sentence condemn the person I most loved in this life to a cold oblivion? If I could have, I wanted to meet this judge and executioner, so I could empty my unrestrained anger upon him. That would have been easier, I believe, than dealing with the deadly abstract entity that was burgeoning inside her.

How do you fight an entity that cowardly hides in the very being of the woman you love? How do you react? How can you help? From my experiences, I can tell you that "being there" with her is the way to help her the most. "Be there" when the diagnosis is given to her. "Be there" when there are decisions to be made after the diagnosis. "Be there" when she gets chemotherapy and/ or radiation therapy. "Be there" for whatever confronts you both, before, during, and after treatment. One thing to remember in all this is, always set aside time for her to sort things out for herself…give her some space for self-healing. One last piece of advice…encourage people to come and visit. This disease takes so much away of its own accord that we do not need to help it by isolating the people affected by cancer. Bring children. They do not need to know the details of your wife's breast cancer…just that the person is sick. I was amazed by the intuitive nature of the children who visited my wife and their unsolicited, unrestrained ways of letting my wife know how they cared and felt. Perhaps, they were the best gifts of all. We still keep the numerous refrigerator artworks she received from the children during that time for people to see. In addition, please…bring yourselves.

The one ting that helped me survive this trying time was to write my emotional discourses into my journals. Sometimes my thoughts and impressions developed into short stories. Other times, I filled pages and pages with disconnected thoughts which, at the time, served to relieve the many tensions I encountered on any particular day. This collection of works was, and is, my way of working through this time of cancer treatment with my wife.

I did not realize, during this time, how involved the caregiver could become in the care of the cancer survivor. The changes the spouse and the family go through have some similar challenges and different outcomes than the breast cancer survivor herself. For a long time, during the cancer experience, I felt though my sanity was slowly slipping away. It was common to experience sudden bursts of tears while driving home from work. Even without any sense of sadness, I would have to stop the car long enough to clear my eyes so I could finish the journey home. Sometimes, while I was alone at our house I would scream, "NO", repeatedly. Other times, I would experience sorrowful wrenching sobs over nothing at all when I was sure no one was around to see me. Later, when I had the chance to speak with other men about their reactions to the diagnosis of their wives' breast cancer, I found them experiencing similar outlets as mine. Before that time, I found little support for men who were confronting breast cancer with their spouses regarding reading material and/or other sources of information. Don't get me wrong, more support systems exist now than when I learned about my wife's breast cancer. Still, there should be more information for men as this phenomenon of increased breast cancer incidence in women continues to grow.

As more and more women are diagnosed with this disease, it will become increasingly important for men to realize that it is alright to feel and act certain ways. As more young women find themselves affected by breast cancer, it will become important for their young husbands and children to understand their roles in dealing with this diagnosis as well. Men must understand that it is okay to sit down with another man and talk about this disease, because that is what it is…a disease. Breast cancer is a disease that affects us all, not just the women in our lives.

In this book, I have used the substance of my experiences as both a spouse and a health care professional to illustrate, with my stories, how devastating this disease can be to family members, spouses, and close friends of breast cancer survivors. In a strange sense, the cancer experience actually enhanced my life in a positive way. You might say, I now stop to smell the roses. Life, for me, is measured in moments, not years. Sometimes you have to live with what life gives you and other times you may get the chance to change things. Cancer marks itself in a cruel irony but leaves in its wake, heroes, warriors, and poets. Come journey into the seasons in cancer with me by traveling through these pages. Even if you never experienced cancer in your life, you may learn something about living from this book.

George S. J. Anderson

The Doorway Into Winter...

"Change can do things to us that makes us different people than the way we were before.."

*"Sometimes we get the chance to change things…"

1993 George S. J. Anderson

Introduction

The "Doorway Into Winter" opened the day we were told my wife had breast cancer. I felt I was peering through a dark doorway associated with concepts of death, loss, isolation, and absolute abandonment of hope. That day, we were unwillingly thrust through this door, which forced us to deal with all the circumstances associated with breast cancer. The specter of death, imminent as the onset of winter in the real world, sat like an unwelcome tenant on the threshold of our existence, threatening our lives together. It was a tangible, ominous presence, which seemed to prognosticate a difficult and perilous journey for my wife. My twelve-year old son and I also felt it draw close to us that day.

"Journeys" is a poem I wrote for my wife about a year after we were married. I ran across it some time after the breast cancer diagnosis became a part of our lives. After reading it again, I realized how poignant the poem really was. As the poem states, we started our lives together after many journeys we had taken alone. Now we put aside the journeys we experienced together to walk hand in hand into the reality of breast cancer and its upcoming treatments.

"Remember This," was written in the months following the diagnosis of breast cancer and its treatment modalities. I originally wrote the story as two journal entries, which I put aside several months before rereading it. Later, I read it again and realized how powerful the entries were. I could not digest the entire story during the first reading, since it stopped me with the strong emotions it unleashed. Eventually, I sat down with it one day and started the painstaking process of editing. When I felt I could do no more with it, I gave it to my wife to read. She thought the story generated such a powerful message that I needed to publish it somehow.

In 1994, I copyrighted the story and self-published "Remember This." The remarks and goodwill the story generated since the first printing have made the efforts worthwhile. However, since 1994, I recognized the story needed some changes to improve the flow of the story. In this version, I have made those changes and I hope you will be as moved as I was as you enter the "Doorway Into Winter."

Journeys

We've been through the shapes of change
    And we shake off the dust of the journey
Come with me and share
    The breath of my living
In an instant we can sail
    To the horizon
With the sails of all the answers
    That lie in whispers
Beneath the pillows of sleep
    With all our dreams
To guide us
    We'll map a course
That we'll follow
    With our waking
And we'll not
    Let a moment
Slip by our eyes
    As we shake off the dust
Of Yesterday
    And share the breath of changing
On our passage
    Through Time

1977 George S. J. Anderson

Remember This

I remember being twelve at this time of year. November, the eleventh month, almost the end, is a turning point in any year. Like this time of year, the age of twelve became that way for me. It may be difficult to see any kind of relationship between being twelve and the month of November, but it is…at least for me.

When I was twelve and the weather took on the vestige of a cold late November, my father took me deer hunting for the first time. We hunted in these mountains when autumn's colored gown, worn like a tapestry of colored leaves, clothed the trees in the early fall. During our previous journeys through the mountain contours, we encountered squirrels, grouse, and other small game in abundance. Now as we walked into this late November hush, the trees seemed like naked bones forced through a discarded cloak of fallen leaves lying on the forest floor.

Our earlier exploits were easily traced since we always hunted within sight of the hewn woodland paths. These paths elaborately quartered large sections of the mountain into easily traversed areas. The mountain paths became safe places where I would not lose my way by wandering away from them. This time was different though. We now deserted those safe mountain paths to walk deeply into the late November foliage and rugged footings of the mountain slopes. We climbed over broken rocks and wind-blown pine trees, travelling to some unknown destination only my father seemed to know.

As he guided me farther into these mysterious woods, I observed strange fantastic places I never saw before. We followed heavily wooded ravines, and crossed over a rocky streambed balancing on a large broken tree lying across it. Finally, we journeyed to the crest of the mountain and stopped near a stand of ancient pines. Within sight of these trees, I saw huge gray-black rocks stained with variegated colors of blue-colored lichen and crowned with patches of crusted green moss. The place was serenely beautiful, a good place to see deer. He instructed me to remain here and hide behind some large trees. He was continuing his journey to meet a group of men already waiting at another part of the mountain. When he arrived there, they were going to start walking through the wooded mountain terrain and drive the deer in my direction. After his instructions, he told me to be very watchful for any deer that might start moving from their extensive drive.

I realized, as he spoke, their walk through this area would be exhausting. I promised him I would be ready as I stationed myself near the trees he pointed our earlier. When he exhausted all the information I needed for the hunt, he left me to join up with the other men. I watched him retreat into the dying brown leaves as he slowly vanished into the underbrush out of view. When I realized I was alone on the crest of this mountain, a cloak of isolation wove itself in the silence and wrapped around me. Like a lone survivor of a lost battalion, I adamantly stood guard, hidden by the large ragged pines with my gun, my winter gear, and thoughts of getting my first buck.

As I waited for the men to begin their drive, I could not help observing the mountain landscape. The simple beauty of the mountain's presence put my mind into a dreamlike state. Thoughts invaded my mind as the cold mountain air began seeping into the skin of my face. Overhead, I sensed the tall pines arching over me like a broken green ceiling of an abandoned cathedral. I felt I was standing in a holy place. My surroundings were primeval, older than the human lives that once inhabited these mountains in ancient times. I wondered how many generations of men might have walked on the stone ledges scarcely detectable beyond my stand. How many ancient people lived and hunted in this place before me?

Many ancient Indian tribes walked and lived in these mountains long before I was born. Now that I had ventured here, I realized they were only shadowy spirits existing in my mind, specters of times long gone from this forested place. These primitive people knew the value of the hunt and only killed what they needed for food. Their tribal hunts were conducted with religious fervor and ceremony. They lived in communion with the forest and believed in the many spirits inhabiting this place. The spirits of the water rushing through the rocky ravines, the spirits silently watching over the tapestry of wooded glens, and the spirits of the pristine mountain air were conceived as living entities. I imagined I could see these tribal hunters in my mind, once again hunting through the area where I now stood, decorated with skins and horns. In my mind, I envisioned one of them clothed in deerskins, wearing the horns of a deer on his head, watching for wild game as he smiled upon me. It felt like a rite of passage to manhood and made me feel at peace with all that surrounded me.

Time passed and child-like thoughts fluttering like soft wings began shaping images in my mind. At the time, I was thinking about what it would be like to get the first deer. I was hoping my deer would be the largest one with the biggest set of horns. It would be fantastic for a twelve-year-old to show up the men in the hunting party! "Here he is…the greatest hunter of the year! He's only twelve and he already has the largest deer we've ever seen!" In a voice coming from behind the men, I heard my dad saying, "Good shooting boy, you really do know how to hunt for deer." However, as I dreamed in this quiet stillness, the cold air began working its way into me. It made me more pensive. Deeper thoughts rooted inside me as I stood there. Childhood dreams, scattered like old abandoned toys, entered my mind.

As a light snow began falling over the mountains, I kept vigil over the rocky terrain and twisted brush that surrounded me. I could still see well enough to make out the details of the terrain and watched as the white flakes worked their magic on the mountainside. The snow was a thin white veil slowly tossed about by the breezes. As I listened, I could hear the snowflakes drop onto the dry brown leaves with a crisp tinkling sound. Away in the distance, I heard the muffled bells of a village church tolling the hour in hushed, reverent tones, stumbling as they passed through the ravines and stony sides of the mountain. The panorama before me awakened old senses and brought back memories of an earlier Christmas in my life. In these memories I dreamed of Santa Claus, and of times and toys I remembered as a small child.

My thoughts drifted back to a time when I believed in Santa Claus, then progressed to another time when I felt devastated because I realized Santa wasn't real. Still, even at the age of twelve, I hoped that some part of Santa Claus lived on inside me. I hoped perhaps I would see the miracles of his work someday, though I knew he didn't exist as my child's mind once believed. Looking out over the mountain, seeing the pines lightly dusted with white, and the snowflakes swirling in gentle swaths of wind, I imagined watching Santa and his reindeer winding off into the sky. For those brief magical seconds, I allowed Santa Claus and Christmas to come alive this one last time. At least the child in me still held onto hope for this coming Christmas. I guess I knew that all things have to change. Living is change. My hopes and doubts of the future awakened within another part of me while the cold mountain air wrestled into my body.

The snow slowed its graceful decent like a dance drawing to a close. Still, some refused to stop and stubbornly continued falling among the trees and rocks. Leaves shuffled in the invisible breeze while branches cracked, rubbing incautiously across their interlocking weave of limbs. All the while, the wind made a low rustling sound as it soughed through the trees. I waited and hoped some deer might wander into the nearby clearings while I continued my musings. I thought, "If this time was the ending of my childhood, then why couldn't I look at my future as it might exist as an adult?" There would be cars, dances, girls, and more school…possibly college. I realized my thoughts merely projected the future before me. But right now, I was simply a twelve-year-old boy sitting on the crest of a mountain with my rifle, waiting…waiting for something to happen. I thought of life being this way. People waiting in lines, people waiting for chances, always waiting… I thought perhaps all this waiting was not what life was all about. Sometimes, things have to matter enough for you to decide and make a choice. You don't always wait. You don't always let the way things are, and the way things were, become the way things always will be. Sometimes you get the chance to change things. Maybe I would get, could get, a chance to do things in a different way. Maybe I would make a difference with my life.

Inside my silent thoughts, I almost missed hearing the heavy foot-like sounds coming up the crest of the mountain. I listened as the restless sound thudded away from me then seemed to stagger toward me again. I caught a glimpse of something passing by some distant mountain laurels. When it came into view I raised my rifle and cocked the hammer. My rifle, a single shot weapon, held only one cartridge before I needed to reload. I knew, from this distance, I would have very little trouble hitting the target. However, I wasn't sure this one shot would bring it down. I hesitated. What stood before me was a four-point buck, cloaked in pure white. I had not yet experienced seeing a buck in the wild, but now, seeing a pure white buck, an albino, as the first deer I ever saw by myself, froze me with indecision.

The white stag merely stood there, looking straight at me. It almost seemed to know its fate when it entered the clearing since it did not attempt any route of escape. In my astonishment I thought, "Was this really a white buck, or a spirit, borne by these ancient mountains?" The seconds seemed longer than time allowed as we stood facing each other. I knew I held the balance of its life in my hands. I began to think it would be a clean kill at this distance. I suddenly had no doubts that I could take its life with this single shot. However, inside I thought, "Would the loss of such a beautiful creature be worth having on my soul?" We both held our stance, enduring these slow-metered seconds, waiting for the other to make a move, deciding which fate would befall us. Finally, I set the hammer back and lowered my gun. The white stag raised its head, as if acknowledging my decision to release it. Realizing our encounter had ended, the deer casually made its way down the side of the mountain. As it moved through the gnarled brush dusted with new-fallen snow, I said to no one in particular, maybe to the spirits of the woods, "Remember this."

I felt I had just experienced something that moved me in a very profound way. I did not completely know or understand how to explain what had just happened. Sometime later, I listened to the approach of the other hunters calling to each other in the woods like ghostly warriors. Their reverberating calls became resounding echoes of reality bringing me back to my senses. I wondered how I would tell my father about the white deer. My father had just asked these men to walk through miles of rough, mountain terrain hoping to chase some deer toward me. I did not believe he would be happy to learn I had simply allowed a deer to walk away. When my father came to get me, he asked if I had seen anything. When I answered him, I told him I had only heard some sounds in the distance and nothing more.

Many things happen in a lifetime that can change us forever. I haven't thought about the hunt with the white stag for a long time. Perhaps in the mind of a twelve-year-old boy the incident repressed itself as a dream, something that never happened. Nevertheless, that time and place remained carved inside my childhood memories as a deeply personal and spiritual encounter. No one else encountered the white stag that year. Even the men who lived in those mountains never reported seeing a white deer any time during that season. I knew I could never disclose the encounter to anyone without risking the ridicule of a twelve-year-old boy with "buck fever." In spite of everything that happened there on the mountain, part of the man I would become started to grow inside me.

Sometimes change comes from out of nowhere and it can do

things to us that make us different people than the way we were before. This year my own son should be going buck hunting for the first time, just as I did so many years ago. That will not happen, however, unless someone takes him other than myself. This year, this November, this time of changes, I was told my wife has breast cancer. Something else has decided her fate. Something else has crept into her life to change it forever. It is something that will change her life and the lives around her.

When my wife and I heard the diagnosis in the surgeon's office, we immediately went cold. All our life emptied out and we felt like hollow shells. We looked out of hollow eyes, and our hearts felt hollow as well. Our dreams shattered and we saw our futures destroyed before our very eyes. Nothing existed for us but grief, sorrow, and oblivion. Nothing can describe how it feels to bear this terrible coldness. It is an empty sensation devoid of colors, warmth, and life itself. It is a challenging desolate frozen despair.

Our afternoon journey from the physician's office to our home passed in silence. Our tears remained suspended in time, too shocked by the news that breast cancer had invaded our lives. When we arrived home and saw our son, all our coldness melted into tears. My wife told our son about her breast cancer through choked tears. I looked upon them as tears washed over my face and over them. We held each other for a long time in the silence and the tears before letting go. When we finally did, I knew a healing would begin. I felt a strength growing from them and from myself. And from somewhere deep inside myself, I felt I needed to pray.

When things hit you from out of nowhere it is difficult knowing where to turn. Cancer is a word, which has connotations of suffering, pain, loss, and eventually death. It was difficult to see beyond that day, beyond the next hour, or beyond the next minute. Time has had very little meaning for us since that day because we try to fit all the living we can into what time we are given. We make each day as if it is our last day together.

One day, soon after the diagnosis, we went to see our lawyer to arrange a time to write her living will and power of attorney. Afterwards, we set up a meeting with our parish priest to administer the "sacrament of the sick" to her. I remembered from my childhood studies, these rites were administered solely to people who were dying. Later, when I became older, it changed to encompass everyone with a serious illness. It was during this time that we finally came to some kind of terms with the diagnosis of breast cancer. We went to church regularly anyway but now it seemed vitally important to be there. Having prepared herself for the chance of dying seemed to strengthen her for this possible chance of living…surviving. Still, I felt something moving deep inside me that I needed to say in a prayer. It took me a long time to remember. Almost a week before Christmas, I finally remembered what I needed to say.

I was standing on our front porch about a week before Christmas admiring the decorations my son and I placed around the house. I was thinking about the fun I shared with him during the Christmas season when he was younger. Santa was alive and well then. As I continued looking over the front lawn, I was thinking how beautiful a little snow would look around some of our pine trees. In my mind, I envisioned how it would almost look like a small replica of the scenery in the mountains. I felt sorry I could not take my son hunting in those mountains where I had hunted as a young man. However, because of his mother's surgery and successive chemotherapy, there wasn't any possibility of my doing so.

Somehow amidst all my fears and confusions concerning the diagnosis of breast cancer, I stumbled across the prayer and hope I was searching for. It must have hidden somewhere in my feelings of regret surrounding this Christmas, or perhaps, I discovered it within the powerful feelings of hope that eventually brought the prayer into my consciousness. When I remembered, it was simply the words, "Remember this."

Perhaps I was bargaining for the impossible. Perhaps it was my way of clinging to something left from my childhood. What I thought of when I said, "Remember this," was releasing the white stag at a time when it could have been my dearest prize. I could have shown this unique prize to the other hunters that would have put them in awe. It was something I could have shown to my father to prove its existence was real and not the fantasy of a twelve-year-old boy. Perhaps what happened that day was something that was meant to be. Something I did in the past now returned to me. What I did that day as a twelve-year-old boy now surfaced as a simple and powerful prayer.

It seems when everything goes wrong we regress to an earlier stage in our life. That is what I felt I might be doing as I recalled the story of the white stag. However, within my memory, I realized that in the moment I could have taken its life, I spared it instead. I remembered how I felt the white stag was the most beautiful creature I had ever seen and I did not have to kill it. I now believe, as I did then, it was the spirit of the mountain that challenged me with a test of manhood, a test which evaluated the worth of my soul. Once I released the white stag, I passed the test. When I passed, I said to the spirit of the mountain, the spirit of the woods, to God, or whatever you believe rules the events of this world, that you must, "Remember this." Perhaps some day will come when I shall have something beautiful, some rare treasure, something of great value to my heart and soul, that I will want spared from the cold mountain of death.

Now, when I pray, I use the words, "Remember this," and hope heaven will indeed remember how a twelve-year-old boy once allowed the white stag to live one cold November morning on those snow-covered mountains. Could heaven do any less? Could God, the spirits of the woods and the mountains do any less than a twelve-year-old boy who spared the white stag? Could this prayer be enough to spare my wife, my white deer, from death? When I pray now, I always say these two words with hopes that they will somehow be carried to one who must hear them. It is my hope. Hope is really all any of us have.

I hope that in the mountains, the ravines, and the valleys dusted with new-fallen snow this Christmas, that a solemn sigh might be heard pushing falling snowflakes within the gentle swaths of wind whispering, "Remember This." Perhaps a church bell will ring in hushed and reverent tones inside the lonely mountain glens, while a child's dreams of Santa Claus and reindeer materialize over the forested mountaintops. Perhaps hope will bring this Christmas alive one more time if we would all just, "Remember this." Perhaps, just like a sound in the distance and nothing more, the white stag will run through the mountain laurels and snowy brush to live another day.

The White Deer

When I finished the first story, *Remember This,* in early 1993, I did not feel as though I left the story complete. A sense of unease surrounded me for quite a long time until one day I picked up my easel and started to draw. What emerged from my efforts was the picture of the white deer.

It seemed after the drawing was completed that I was finally able to move away from the story and the picture and move onto other things. Some time later a friend asked me if I had drawn the picture a certain way on purpose. He asked me if I had noticed that everything around the deer was either dead or dying and the only thing of life in the picture was the white deer. After closer inspection I realized that what he was saying was true. I guess my subconscious was working through my artistic abilities when I drew the picture.

The completed drawing now resides in the office of the York Cancer Center in York, Pennsylvania.

Drawing by,
George S. J. Anderson   1993

Beneath the Promises of Spring...

"The sound was like a ghost scratching out words of last summer's glory, letting spring know it can have aspirations to dream of better things, better times, that life comes out of ashes, and not to forget."

"Tears are like "nails of life."

1995-1996 George S. J. Anderson

Introduction

Before any spring can come into existence, a reckoning of sorts must be made. The past of last summer's glory relegates itself to ashes giving spring the inner strength to move on to its own distinct time and beauty. These principles have existed since there have been seasons written upon this earth. Poets, prophets, evangelists, and artists have discussed, written tales, and illustrated nature's seasonal passages from the time words were inscribed and visions captured in canvases, books, poetry, and all other manners of artistry.

In this early springtime, several months after her diagnosis, I found myself involved in the processes of breast cancer treatments in-depth with my wife. Before Christmas of the past year, my wife lost all her hair to her first chemotherapy treatment. With the loss of her hair, it became overwhelmingly evident that she was a survivor of a devastating illness whose outcome was not entirely predictable. Though my stories are written to accentuate the case in point, breast cancer being the point here, not everything in my life revolved around the care of my wife during this time. I still had to function in my position as a registered nurse during the night hours. I still had to function as a father to my then thirteen-year-old son at our home. I had the added responsibilities of being caregiver to my wife and filling in wherever it became necessary in the operations of our home. All of this was very tiring and I had to rely on help from wherever I could get it. Many times my waking hours were strictly dedicated to organizing everything, everybody, and realizing my own resources.

We have many friends and relatives in the area where we live. We were certainly most blessed when the time came to get help. Many people did not know what to do to help us and I certainly did not know what to tell them. One of the neatest, most appreciated things that happened was when our friends and relatives brought hot meals for us. So many times, food was the last thing I wanted to think about when coming back from a session of chemo or a particularly "bad hair day," (no pun intended). It made those times more bearable and helped all of us deal with what was happening in a more positive frame of mind. For that, I want to send them special thanks.

As I said before, my life did not stop because my wife had breast cancer. Yes, people stopped me and asked me how she was doing. They asked me about her chances of survival. They wanted to know how treatment was going and if they could do anything to help the family. There was a great show of concern at my workplace and at hers as well. They sent us flowers, tons of flowers, so many that my home was a literal garden in the middle of January. We appreciated all of it. My wife kept all the cards that came with the flowers and even now reads them on days when she gets "the blues." She says it helps her remember there are so many people out there pulling for her. Still, my work was my work and I had to leave my problems at home stay there. I had to deal with all types of patients in my workplace, including patients with breast cancer. Though in my heart, I would have preferred not to do so.

Beneath the promises of spring lie the ashes of the past. In the story "Underneath," I explore this time during my wife's breast cancer treatment in relation to the many breast cancer situations I participated in during the same interval. Though it was a difficult and terrible time for me, the experiences intensified how important it is to find better ways to treat this disease. Perhaps a call for a cure is not so irrational once you realize this disease has been a part of the female population since the times the Great Pyramids of Egypt were built. Yes, even there you will find documentation of breast cancer by these ancient physicians. Imagine, thousands of years of knowledge of this disease and only a few decades worth of treatment. I believe it is time women were given their due. Isn't it time to get this disease relegated to the past?

In June of 1995, my wife's breast cancer support group wanted a poem written for a ceremony in which they dedicated a weeping cherry tree to the surviving members of the support group. The weeping cherry tree was chosen because of its pink blossoms, (Pink being the color of breast cancer awareness), and because of the tree's graceful branches which represent the reaching out to one another for support. Though the poem was not used during the ceremony in its completed form, I included the entire poem in this work for you to enjoy.

The poem was originally titled "Daughters of Eve." However, since the stanza that suggested the inference to the title was not used in the dedication, it was renamed "Litany of Hope."

Litany of Hope

Watch as the wind whispers
   Through these willowy stems…
      They are Survivors,
         With softly bending branches,

Kneeling in silent prayer…
   Leaves like clasped hands
      Unfold Spring-pink blossoms
         Held like a rosary of hearts

That sing out
   With their Litany
      Of Hope…

Daughters of Eve,
   The challenge of the Wind
      Has called you
         To this urgent Cause…

With your hopes
   And yearning hearts
      Upon the wild Wind's roar
         Send your prayers

Blowing like pink petals
   Over Eden's Door…

1995 George S. J. Anderson

Underneath

I never heard her song… Through the hollow black tubes came the sound of air moving, rushing in and out. As the leading edge of the metal disk landed like an alien craft upon the bony ridges stretching out like ripples of sand, I listened. Again the strange metal disk moved near a fleshy swell on this human landscape and again I listened to the sounds underneath. I heard the muffled "thump-thush" of a failing heart. I visually counted ribs there on the exposed flesh. My eyes examined the course of a silver-white line where a breast was obviously omitted. It was a line accented as a final punctuation mark inscribed in flesh. I looked in wonder, as my realization to understanding surfaced that this lost swell of tissue was an effort in vain too late to save her. In a silent homily of my own, I issued a quiet prayer for my own wife also numbered among those afflicted with breast cancer.

I pushed the silver disk across this devastated land and heard the shallow breathing, the internal sound, the ever-present heartbeat that says you are "alive." However, deep inside myself I asked, "Are you living?" I never heard her song so I did not feel I had the right to ask out loud. I closed my eyes and imagined the one cell dividing repeatedly, one after another, tumor cells rampantly growing larger in the dark and hidden silence. This cancer was burgeoning in the midst of the body sounds that grew steadily more silent as each cell split again and slowly continued stealing the remaining tiny pieces of her life. Eventually cancer would kill the song that masked its silent progress. How can you understand this marvel named "cancer" when all it requires is life to live itself? How do you understand the purpose of cancer when at the peak of its life, another life ends, ending the existence of the cancer as well? Cancer marks itself in a cruel irony. Underneath the cancer was turning her into a sacrificial casualty marked into the records as statistical data…not viable. I felt the shudder in her breathing and opened my eyes.

My hands touched the porcelain skin, yellowed in places like tallow. I pushed the other breast away with one hand, proffered then refused, so the alien disk might hear and offer counsel on how long, how much suffering was left to endure as the life leeched out of her body. The metal disk went sliding down as it listened to the elemental sounds of the abdomen. These sounds were the machinery works that linked her body to our reality of a living world. With this music silenced, her time in this closed reality became shorter, more precious in its passing moments. The disk returned to my shoulder like a well-trained animal and laid there caught by the tubes encircling my neck like a pair of black snakes.

I started to feel with my hands, these tools evolved to see where my eyes cannot, flesh upon flesh finishing this tragic journey. Examining her ankles, I met the swelling that I feared to find. Though I had discovered it before, I somehow hoped it would be miraculously gone when I checked again. I applied pressure and I felt my fingers swallowed into flesh swollen with fluids the body could no longer remove. As I felt this I thought of the ocean tides of the world ebbing and rising as the world revolved around the sun, spinning on its axis, and the moon rotating around the earth. Mother earth involuntarily chose this way to move the great water basins of the earth, preventing them from deadly stagnation. Water must be moving to sustain life, once it stops, life stops. As I felt this in her ankles, I wondered if cancer erased all her memories about the rises and falls of the tides in her body. I thought if somehow she remembered, perhaps her world could revolve again, the moon could move about, and the tides would return to their normal ways. In her world though, all things were slowing down, coming to an end, a stop, a completion.

I replaced the obligatory cotton gown and pulled the covers over her swollen discolored feet. My cursory evaluation was completed. I looked towards her husband who was huddled in a chair by the bedside. His eyes were haunted with the pain of his emotions, pleading that my news was something he could endure. I told him, "Not much has happened since I last checked." He nodded, clasped his hands in his lap, and escaped into that silent reverie where prayers are launched into silent darkness. If "hope" exists here, it is the fervent hope that no one else will enter the domain this room represents too soon.

I knew this place. Perhaps I realized, more than her husband, that she was not the first to enter this room as an unguarded prisoner. I knew the only door open to her was through a corridor of humbling pain. It was my job to ward off the pain, to walk her to the end of the corridor, and let her open the final door out of this lonely prison. It is dying with dignity that makes this process endurable. Though death was not welcome, it may come this time as a friend offering peace from the pain and suffering.

As I stood in the doorway, I turned momentarily and looked back into the room. I listened for her song and could not hear it. Instead I heard the silent sorrow and fateful call from the land of the dead beckoning her to the other side of the door. Underneath it all, I sensed my own fear of the inevitable…that we all die. Before I turned away again, looking through that portal leading to the hallway, to a place where time pretended to go on at its normal pace, I spoke to the man in the chair. "I'll be back in a little while to check in on her." I said these words like a solemn incantation, with hopes of doing so might lessen the blow, lessen the pain of losing her, when I knew underneath it would not. A tightness arose in my throat and all my words seemed to dry up as I realized how pointless this effort was. He nodded in affirmation that he had heard me but his eyes never left her face as if by turning away he might lose some future memory of this sadness.

I turned and walked away from this place into the corridor to other rooms and other stories unfolding. Outside the walls held vigil while the night sky watched over us. Against the windowpanes, from some of the rooms, I could hear the stirring of the night wind picking up pace from time to time. The wind blew the silent naked branches and dried leaves like winter's ashes against the glass windowpanes. The sound was like a ghost scratching out words of last summer's glory, letting spring know that it could have aspirations to dream of better things, better times, that life comes out of ashes, and not to forget.

As I turned into the hall past other stories, other rooms, the low chatter of the other nurses and patients seemed to be, "How is the lady at the end of the hall?" I listened but simply heard the same frightened echoes in their questions. "Is death walking this close to us?" "Will death pass over our doorways while we are asleep?" "Will we know when death has come tonight?" I heard their fear. I felt their concerns and their helplessness over death. Underneath it all, I felt their sadness as this parting drew close to us all. We hardly knew her, yet soon she would be leaving on her final journey. Her silent footsteps were already fading into the hallway to that final door. We never heard her song, but we tried to listen through the silence anyway.

The nurses' station blazing with its large florescent lights seemed cold, sterile. I assembled my newfound data and scratched out words upon the paper pages that had become her life now. I wrote inadequate words to describe and define the presence of the woman who was once a viable human presence now being stretched like a gossamer thread between this existence and the next. How do you write words to describe a life? What words adequately define the passing of souls, the parting of spirits? I listened through the charged air of chatter and the rustling wind outside the windows. Within the sounds began the pattering of rain splashing against the windows. The rain hastened my writings while I transiently watched the world through the wet panes of glass.

Through the colorless windowpanes, I witnessed a collection of water droplets slide down the flat glass. Some moved slowly, others were rushing to meet the bottom of the glass. I thought, "This rain will nurture the earth and give it strength to move on." In the darkness, on the perimeters of the outside lighted thoroughfares, I saw the outlines of trees. Nestled there in the darkness with the rain sheeting upon them they appeared as shining black, reflections of light on the craggy wet bark. The wind continued to sluice through the rain, blowing it carelessly against the glass almost like tears. As I watched, I wondered what I would say to her husband as she drew her final breath. Would there be words, adequate words? The shadows of these questions darkened the outposts of my being more than once. They were the same questions asked by different authors yet the answers were still unfulfilling, empty in their worth.

The smell of coffee invaded the air around me. I went into the kitchen adjoining the station and poured a cup. I thought again of the woman at the end of the hall and poured a second cup for her husband. I left the first cup sitting like an orphaned child by the coffeepot then walked slowly down the corridor. I entered the room where the man was sitting in a chair mesmerized by the labored breathing of the woman on the bed. He was holding one of her hands clasped between both of his. He looked up at me as I realized I had intruded upon some tender moment between them. "I brought you some coffee…I didn't know how you liked it…"

He thanked me, told me what he liked in his coffee, and went on staring into the face of his wife unblinking. I turned and left this tender moment between them then sent a mental note to myself to come back a little later.

Upon returning to the kitchen, I found the lone cup I left for myself sitting on the counter near the coffeepot. I picked it up and drained half of it down my throat then started pouring the rest down the sink. I had no taste for it at the moment. I have been troubled with insomnia lately and I thought it might be my coffee intake. I poured the coffee away, coating the sink's steel bowl with it. Almost as an afterthought, I rinsed the coffee down the drain thinking that underneath there are other reasons for not sleeping besides the coffee. I picked up the other cup meant for her husband and fixed it the way he asked. I turned the corner to the hall with the coffee then noticed the call light glowing over the door at the end of the hall. When I saw it, I realized her shadowy spirit was sliding slowly away. I wondered how many would count themselves among those who could bear witness to her passing.

I hurried back to the room almost spilling the coffee I was trying to carry. I entered the grim doorway and noticed an almost palpable change had crept into the room. I felt it on my skin, as it was almost as real as the pungent cancer smell I breathed near the dying woman. The man did not seem to sense this and appeared unaffected by it as I observed him stooping over the bed with tears running out of his eyes. He said to me. "She just started doing this…I thought I should call." I pulled my stethoscope from my shoulder and listened, though it was very apparent that her condition had become grave now. It was obvious that her breathing pattern had deteriorated and her time here was stealing away quickly. Underneath I could feel her moving to that door at the end of the hall. Final notes in a symphony called life were being played on the cadence of her harsh labored breathing. A song was fading, a song I never heard.

I said to him, " Is there anyone you want me to call?" He looked at me with his pleading eyes and I knew and felt his heart breaking. He wanted to say something to me but there were no words within this spoken language that could possibly express the feelings we both sensed in each other. We saw each other as spirits holding onto this plane of corporeal states. I realized and understood that there were others not present here who needed to say goodbye to her. Though he was not capable of acknowledging me now, I accepted the lead and with gentle words communicated to him I would call his family to come in. He nodded in silent agreement then with resignation or possible acceptance he sat, almost knelt, within the chair beside the bed like a reverent genuflection.

I hurried from the room and made the urgent calls using bits of magic ebbing and flowing through the fine wires crying out in the darkness in search of solace for this grieving man. I heard the ringing on the other ends of the wires, then I heard a rush like air moving in hollow tubes, then there were voices sounding urgent and questioning. I issued my pleas into their ears like bitter news…They are coming. Others are coming to wait for and witness this passing.

After the calls go out, I alert the other nurses to watch for these benevolent wayfarers and send these witnesses to the room at the end of the hall. After I have made these arrangements with the staff, I returned to the room with the man and the dying woman. I told him that others were journeying here and would soon arrive. He asked me if I would check her again and I told him that I would. Though underneath I knew I would hear the sounds of dying breathing, feel the stagnant pools of water, see the pain of dying, and smell the pungent odor of cancer lingering in the room near her body. He watched me closely as if he was my mentor and I was his student. While I was doing my assessment he asked, "Is she close?"

In my mind, the question he posed was actually many questions with so many feelings, beliefs, and pain in them that I had to think awhile before I could answer him. I could hear some of the questions in my head as I stretched into the horizons of knowledge to find some answers. In my mind I heard, "How long does she have?" I could never answer this question because no one really knows just how long a person has. Experience has taught me not to guess, but people still think nurses and doctors can divine the hour that a person passes away. Sometimes we can get close but most times a greater power than any of us dictates the time.

I faintly heard another question in the wringing of his hands, "Is she in pain now that she cannot tell us?" Again I did not know the real answer to this but I hoped that she was not in pain and to that end, I continued to medicate her hourly just to be sure. I always thought it was the right thing to do to keep cancer patients out of pain.

Then in his pleading eyes I see the final question of a man standing alone in a room with his dying wife and a total stranger. "Will the family make it in time?" To that end I have done all I could do in these dark morning hours to put out a call to all those who had heard her song in their lifetimes. Sometimes I have seen the dying person hold on until all the family members make it to say goodbye to them. Other times the dying person has already said goodbye to all those that were dear to them and simply slip away in a quiet moment when everyone has gone out of the room. I never really heard their songs so I never knew how they would end their melody.

He was too distraught to ask me what he really wanted to know so I simply said, "I think she is close now but I think she will hold on until your family gets here." In his humanity, I saw the tears borne in his eyes, travelers across the skin of his face, beginnings and endings, meetings and partings, like a roadmap of the tales and legends of his life with this great woman. He caught himself crying in front of me and vainly tried to stop. He was embarrassed and said; "I'm sorry for crying…it's just…" and he trailed off into silence.

I think something broke inside me then. I don't know if it was because I saw myself in him. My own wife was also diagnosed with breast cancer. I knew very well that I could be in this same room or one like it sometime. I think, perhaps, I did see this man as my mentor. He was showing me what could be in store for me and it was making me stronger for knowing it. I looked at the window partly visible between the partially drawn shades and watched as the wind slapped the rain against the window. The droplets ran down the windowpanes in silent torrents. From somewhere deep inside me words formed, thoughts created their magic, and my tongue loosened so that I was again able to say something…anything. Words welled up inside me and I delivered them with an eloquence of which I did not believe I was capable.

I looked across the room from the side of the bed and said, "Your tears are like 'nails of life.' They betray us with these crystal emblems of courage that tell us we have loved someone. Do not hide your tears because you are ashamed, or embarrassed, or because you think they show weakness. Tears are borne of courage, not cowardice. They show the worth of your love for someone. If we have not the courage to love then tears would not exist. There would be no passion or depth to this life. Life would be superficial, meaningless. When you are moved so deeply there are tears, then something of great importance happened to you. Something mattered to you, moved you, changed you for some purpose you may not even be aware of at the time. Tears are the "nails of life." When someone we love has gone, they leave us our tears. If that love was great, then sorrow stays with us a little longer than it would have if that love was not. Tears do not come easy to us because they were earned with love. Like a nail, they allow us to build some new dimension to our life if we would only take them and use them that way. Otherwise, we leave a dimension of ourselves undone because we do not know or understand it. In our sorrow a loved one leaves us these nails with which to build. To choose not to build is to wallow in the nails, never seeing the greater part of what a loved one left us. Nails like these become bitter knives that cut us, pierce us, and leave us in pain. Many never see them as an implement to a greater good, a better state of being, or a deeper, richer understanding of life. Instead their tears become a reminder of a great loss. They become blinded by them, never seeing the potential good in sorrow's tears and building with 'living nails'."

My emotional dissertation was finished. The man who had asked me to forgive him for crying walked over and embraced me. He thanked me for all my help and said he would think about what I had said. The tears were still running down his cheeks but even in his sorrow, he smiled at me. All the irony in the world spoke on that face without a single pronounced word to define it. I wondered if anything I said would help at all. However, as he waved at me through the doorway I felt a strange sense of relief, a lifting of heaviness from the room. Underneath I knew he would be alright now. I never heard her song, but for a moment I think a low single note hovered about me while looking into the eyes of the man standing beside her. She was not gone. Others knew parts of her melody and could sing it from their hearts. Underneath I knew her song would not die in this room. It would not be lost in the hush of raindrops falling outside her window this early spring morning.

As he turned away from me, my thoughts became introspective as I recalled a familiar place. In my mind, I returned to a favorite room at my home. It was here where my memories silently transported me. Here my memories of a grandfather clock patiently standing guard over time's relentless journey deposited me. Within my memories, I watched as it chimed away the passing hours, gracefully measuring the time we spent pursuing that which was valuable to us. I realized when this clock became a presence in our home, it discretely intertwined into the fabric of our life's background. Eventually, I took this splendid clock for granted. I knew it would always be there, chiming, speaking its voice in the quiet solemn air, while the slow persistent heartbeat of the pendulum continued measuring the hours away. One day, while perceiving the time on another clock, I realized our grandfather clock would soon be chiming the hour. I listened a while but the chimes never sounded. Curious, I went into the living room and investigated what had gone wrong. By reading the time on the face of the grandfather clock, it became apparent that the clock stopped running during the time I had been asleep.

It seemed strange that I had allowed so many hours to slip by without ever missing the sound of it chiming the hours away. Looking inside, the pendulum sat still like a mechanical heartbeat gone dead. Somehow, this sense of finality sent a chill through me. Silence filled the room now that I realized this device had stopped. I opened all the doors to the clock and tried everything I knew to restart it. Nothing helped. The clock would not run in spite of everything I tried. Eventually, I ended up calling the clocksmith to fix it.

During the next week, while the clocksmith repaired the clock, I began to realize how much I missed hearing its chimes. I remembered lying in bed one night thinking that I should get up when I heard the clock chime the morning's hour. When the hour finally came, I bolted out of bed in the deafening silence. The clock had failed. I had forgotten it was still not working. My wife wondered what was wrong with me when I realized what had happened. It took me a little while getting used to its absence that week. Eventually, the clock was repaired and our activities returned to their previous ways. This happened before the words "breast cancer" entered our lives and our home.

It's funny how superstitions get started. I don't believe in them as a rule, but when you are dealing with a deadly disease like cancer, you sometimes do things that are a little strange. I guess this was how my superstition with the clock started.

One day, during the time my wife stayed in the hospital for her mastectomy, I returned home a few minutes before the hour. As I got inside the door, I laid my coat over the back of the chair. Subconsciously, I was listening for the chimes when they failed again. I walked towards the clock and realized what had happened. Because of all the demands of cancer treatment, running the house, getting my son off to school, hospital visits, and overnight trips to his grandparents, I missed pulling the weights up on the clock. At that moment, I was alone in the house. Seeing the clock sitting lifeless with the gravity weights expended made me numb. Somehow, the irony of the stopped clock and the way our lives seemed to have stopped due to cancer put a chill through me. I opened the lower door where the weights were located and pulled them up. I restarted the pendulum, set the clock, and waited for the next hour to strike. The clock has been running since that time.

Somewhere inside all of us, dark places reside keeping our fears alive. When our fears are too much to live with, I believe we put them into terms we can function with. We place them deep inside the marrow we call "ourselves." Sometimes those terms become places where superstitions are borne and lie in wait. Since the day the clock stopped, I have been implacable with keeping it running. It was almost as though the motionless clock could cause the cancer to come back and eventually claim her life. My fears linger inside that dark place as long as I sustain its operations. Call it fear. Call it superstition if you will. As of this time, I have not allowed the clock to stop running. When we leave for extended periods of time I have someone bring in our mail, check our telephone messages, water the plants, look the house over, and pull up the weights on the clock. As a sentinel over our lives, it tirelessly counts the hours, minutes, and seconds of our lives together.

As I watched this man and woman struggling with their last moments together, I thought back on the grandfather clock and hoped in my absence it had not run down. Their time together was drawing to a close. Their invisible clock nearly grounded out as it shed its precious seconds waiting for relatives and loved ones to arrive. Which would happen first? Would their clock sound her final hour before her loved ones arrived, or would they make it in time to share what was left of her waning life?

I now saw this room for what it really was…a prison guarding what little life remained in her like a holy sanctuary. Watching their struggle unfold before me made me think how small the spaces are that we pass our lives in. We seem to live inside these walls while outside the world rages at us with storms, winds, and rains.

Outside this room, a real world exists…not in rooms like this one. What laws have governed us to pass our lives in such confined places? We are born in rooms, live our lives in rooms stacked like cubes within cubes. Now this man and this woman would say goodbye here while outside the wind tried to rip away at the walls that so confined us. It had no effect. We have become too proficient at building these walls and better yet at living inside them. They are places to be in but never really allow us to be in place. It is times like these when I wanted to tear the outside walls down and let the wind, the rain, and the elements of the earth visit upon us, welcoming them like friends we never knew.

Trying to be part of them one more time before the last spark of earthly life faded into that final darkness.

Finally, the wet, sorrowful travelers began to arrive on the unit. The nurses meet them at the desk and have them come to the room. As more and more witnesses arrive, they follow in silent procession to the room at the end of the hall. I wonder what it is they hope to see, to do, to say, that may soften these last harsh moments of her life. Underneath, I realize they are only what they seem to be, witnesses to this passing.

As I watched with them, I felt like a necessary intruder. Here were all the people who had listened to her song. They knew it in their hearts and mine was never part of it. Still, they seemed to need my guidance through this time as we all stood or sat watching this last chapter unfold before us.

One shuddered breath followed another. Underneath they sounded like whispers or beckoning prayers moving her closer to that final door. I watched with them as she took one final labored breath and left it fall out in utter silence. Her fingers tightened then dripped over the edge of the mattress in an almost symbolic gesture, releasing life. The final doorway had been passed and she could finally move away from this corporeal state, this room, and fly beyond these rooms that still confined the rest of us.

With the realization that she was gone, the family wept. Somber embraces, hands touched, eloquent passions for the dead were shared and gave strength to those who could not yet fathom her passing. I gave condolences to all present, then left the room, giving them that time alone all people require to say goodbye. I never heard her song. Now it was gone forever, only to be sung by the ones who truly loved and knew her. I had to wonder how many lives were cut short by this disease called "breast cancer." To see this much pain inflicted made me that much more insistent to help anyone I could with a diagnosis like this. At that moment, I hated this disease.

Finally the family emerged from the room and thanked us all for what we had done for their mother, sister, daughter, and wife. This woman had so many roles but I realized that all women could have fit into any one of these roles or all of them. Knowing this made me sad to know just how vulnerable women are to this disease simply because they are women. There was no equality to it. No sense of fairness. Breast cancer did not deal with fairness, or with rules, or even with gender. We are all susceptible to it with the "lion's share" of the disease going to women.

Somehow the time must come to win back some of the lives lost to breast cancer. I wanted this day to be the one.

I watched as the family filtered off the floor leaving just her husband behind. We spoke of final arrangements, belongings, and other trivial matters. He asked me to walk back to the room with him so he could say his last goodbye. We left the station in silence traveling into the dimly lighted room. Inside this room, she appeared as merely a peaceful sleeper. He walked to her side, bent down, then brushed a lock of her hair from her forehead and kissed her. He told her goodbye then asked me to take care of her from there. I told him to go home and get some rest though underneath I knew it was not something he was likely to do. As he turned slowly away to leave this room a final time I said, "Surely she at peace now...in a place much better than this." He nodded his agreement and said he believed this as well considering the purgatory she went through in the process of dying. I watched as he finally left the room to go home, leaving the empty repository that once held the life he most loved with me. This song was finally over. It would never again trip down the lonely hollows of his heart or fly into his arms to be caressed. Here there was only silence.

I prepared the body then left her alone in the room. I realized when we are no longer a resident of this place we leave our houses behind. Houses stand as a collection of rooms, a tangible reminder of who we were. Just like these rooms, her physical body remained as a physical reminder of who she was, how she lived, and what she was all about in her lifetime. It was a memorial of empty rooms, empty glass windows, and distant places where her life was played out in metered intervals. It was a place where word were spoken, music played, songs were sung into the air, and finally intervals of silence. It was in these moments of silence where she might have listened to the voices of her ancestors. Now, at this moment, she was there with them smiling down on all of us.

Outside the rain had stopped and a pleasant breeze was blowing against the windows sending the last of the raindrops huddled on the glass to the lower sill. They seemed like tears that were drying up. As I filled out the papers, called all the arranged attendants and physicians, I wondered what the woman at the end of the hall was like when she was alive and in good health. Underneath I wished her well in her final journey and hoped her family would survive without her.

When everything for her was completed, I realized my shift

was just about over. I looked back over the busy nurse's station and realized how everything had returned to the way that it was. Watching everything bustling and moving made me think how little impact this woman's passing had on all of us. Lives moved on. We touched, we listened, and nothing seemed to change us. Underneath I secretly wanted her life to count for more than a mere statistic. Somehow she had passed through all but a few of our lives and we never heard her song.

I picked up my coat and the few belongings I carry to work each night and followed the corridor to the outside world. As I walked through morning's door, I was immersed in the early glow of light mixing with the tourmaline and emerald colors from the wet dewy grass. Sprays of light poured beams drifting through the naked winter woods touching pristine green waiting to be born. Nature, tender in its innocence, borne from the harsh lands of winter, made me drunk with the intensity of its nectar. I walked a short distance away from the buildings towards the parking lot and the well-groomed gardens tended by unseen hands. I left anxiety and fear standing on the sidewalk in the shadows where they gazed like hungry specters waiting for another repast of frightened souls.

I never heard her song but the intensity of the spring day that confronted me made me feel the immense power life presented. I was in wonder of all that surrounded me. I almost sensed her presence near me, though certainly it was just a feeling that lingered in the early morning mists on this spring day. I felt a subtle breeze fill the humid air around me. It stirred the dry dead leaves at my feet, burdens of last winter's memories. Within the breeze a sound, like a song, whispered in tune with what surrounded me on all sides. It was abundant with life, imbued with bright promise and hope.

It seemed I was walking on "the road less traveled" that morning. I never heard her song but it was not from loss of hope. I realized I was not meant to hear her song in my lifetime. I would never hear her song because she only allowed the poetry of her life to remain behind. They are the words underneath the song and we are all a part of her hope. For you see, we sing her song for her because that is her hope and ours as well. All our songs, together, blending like the light in morning's door, the threshold of this life and the next, the bright sounds, the dark skies, all voices together…they are our song.

As the morning light grasped the colors of the early spring's hyacinth and sweet-smelling honeysuckle, I realized that we were all witnesses to this life and in the end, underneath it all, we were all like a song. I listened to the wind stirring in the leaves then heard it fade with a final harmony in its journey to the sky, to a place where all the hymns of life grow silent. I never heard her song but in the wake of her departure, she touched me. Where she touched, she left some tears, something for me to take as "living nails" and build something more to my self that I never had…underneath.

Completion

This drawing shows the anguish of the mate of the woman with breast cancer. The picture was inspired by a dream in which there were steps, or rungs, of light crossing left to right with more vertical lines in tangent with them. Within these rungs was a woman who had lost a breast and a man who offered his heart to replace it. Later when I tried to put the image onto paper I added the geometrical models onto the paper. The models represent basic drawing designs used to create body shapes. I felt these shapes were important to the drawing in that as the man was trying to complete the woman's loss, the shapes existed to complete each of them.

Drawing by,
George S. J. Anderson   1999

Inside a Summer's dream

**"To do this you must survive change
…then you can truly live."**

**"You begin to appreciate a drop of water
and are awed by an ocean."**

1995-1996 George S. J. Anderson

Introduction

Over a year and a half passed since the initial diagnosis of breast cancer. This was when my insomnia began. The onset was slow, subtle, and eventually I had tremendous difficulty staying asleep for more than a few hours a day. During the time I experienced these bouts with insomnia, my wife was enjoying her first three month interval of not seeing a doctor, for one reason or another, in almost eighteen months. Before this time, she was seeing at least one of her three or four physicians once a month. Though her physicians had nothing less than the best intentions for her, their presence in her life only served to remind her she was actively battling cancer. Since they were stepping back, she now began to realize she had survived both the cancer and the cancer treatment.

She was encouraged she had endured these breast cancer treatments long enough to persevere as a survivor. I wanted to support her renewed vigor for life as much as I could. I did not want her worrying about our son or myself during this placid interval. I wanted this peaceful time to be her time to heal, to regain some of the lost pieces of her life. I certainly did not want to distract her recovery with problems of my own. Actually at the time this was happening, I did not really feel I had a problem.

While she used her time to rebuild some normalcy in her life and regain some of the strength she lost during her struggles with cancer treatment, I was losing more and more sleep. When my insomnia was at its peak, I was sleeping two hours a day for over a month. During that time, I was tormented by bizarre and sometimes terrible dreams. I remembered reading about Freud and his interpretations of dreams. Considering what I read and the caliber of the dreams I was having, I began to believe I was starting to go clinically insane. I felt ready to release my tenuous hold of reality and allow the lunacy of these dreams wash my sensibilities away. Or, I could simply permit them to effect their course until they stopped. It was during this time, while the dreams raged in my mind, that an incredible revelation occurred to me. As I continued to have this dream repeatedly, I began breaking the pattern of my insomnia. I eventually saw my family doctor for medical help with the insomnia, but it was the dream that helped me survive this time.

The story, called "The Merlin Dream," written after my experiences with insomnia were long past, had no basis in reality, other than my dreams and my inner self. I feel it was perhaps the most difficult story I had to put down on paper. I had to rely entirely on my recollections of the dream which, by the time I started to write it down, were mere ghosts of my memories. In spite of everything I encountered in this process, I was able to recreate my dream as a story. It took approximately a year to organize my thoughts and make some sense of the chaotic memories, but I believe this effort may give the reader some insight into the depth from which dream originated. Inside this summer's dream you may soon realize the incredible potential a person has to heal from within…even when you don't truly understand how much healing you need.

Daydream Life

When you were younger
Remember how your elders would say
That you would do so much better
Than they ever did
Then you had your whole
Life to live
Now you are older
Trying to be wiser
Never did build your
Palaces in the clouds
And as you sit here thinking
About when you get started
How things will be
Thinking you are wiser
You stare out a window
In
A Dream

1983 George S. J. Anderson

The Merlin Dream

"Do you believe in the Once and Future King?" Merlin asked, as his trenchant hypnotic gaze dissected me from any semblance of reality I might have had. He appeared in this dream as he did before, resembling a great owl with its feathered wings radiating with a blue spectral light. The effect of his manifestation flowed like a dance of bright emanations caught within the flames of a blue fire stone crowning the handle of the crystal sword clutched in its talons. After his typical dramatic entry, he callously metamorphasized before me. He restructured as the great magician of legendary tales, wrapped in flowing black velvet robes. His rainments, encrusted with gold and diamonds, resembled the night sky's constellations. A thick fog curled about us while its tendrils captured the variegated hues of blue imprisoned by the glowing hilt of the sword. About us, the forest rose in naked branches clothed only with tatters of the harsh autumn air and torn cloak of fog. Again, we would wrestle in the worlds of restless sleep and troubled dreams.

This is the Merlin Dream. Its haunting presence overshadows me since my wife's diagnosis with breast cancer. I realized many changes inherent to the diagnosis of breast cancer would affect her life. However, I never looked into that mirror centered within my mind's eye to observe what was happening to me. My heart felt her fear as she did. My eyes watched her life's flame diminish to almost nothing then, almost magically, I watched her rekindle a spark that became the fires by which she would fight. I was never certain if she would survive this battle. I was reticent to understand it was not a battle I could fight for her. It enraged me to know I was left with such impotent weapons against this devastating foe. My only true weapon was my outstretched hand and my presence; otherwise, I was only a witness to her struggles with cancer treatment.

At night, while the world was asleep, I worked as a registered nurse on a medical surgical unit. Here I had the responsibility to care for a woman also diagnosed with breast cancer during the time my wife was undergoing her own battles with cancer treatment. She was diagnosed about a year before my wife's cancer was discovered. She had entered the final, terminal stages of cancer. Her cancer had metastasized to the bones and caused her a great deal of pain. We medicated her as much as we were able and eventually she merely existed, silenced by the medication that staved off the pain. As a registered nurse, it was my duty to care for people suffering with all types of cancer at one time or another.

On my unit, the word "cancer" became a commonplace term. It was a word we tossed about carelessly among ourselves. "Cancer" was not a word I ever thought would travel home with me. Now, through these women's struggles with life and death, cancer assaulted me in both my home and in my workplace. These two women were diagnosed with breast cancer. Both were about the same age. One was dying. One was fighting for her life.

Eventually, the woman I cared for at my workplace died. It made a significant impact on my life and made me respect the severity of this disease with renewed fervor. I guess, subconsciously, it affected me in ways I might not ever completely realize or understand either now or in the time that existed.

My wife was diagnosed with a stage III breast cancer. As a nurse, I understood the implications of the diagnosis. It meant, at that time, her chances for a five-year survival were less than forty percent. To say the cancer diagnosis made us look at our own mortality would almost be a "cliché." I imagined the concept of cancer as an hourglass that had been sitting on a dusty shelf somewhere in the compartments of her body. For some reason, no one would ever know, that hourglass was turned over spilling the first grain of sand into the lower glass chamber like the first cancer cell starting in her body. With the lower chamber filling with sand, I watched her body filling with cancer cells. The only way to stop the progression was to turn the hourglass over again, making the sand reverse itself, giving us time. I was afraid no one could turn that hourglass over as the sand continued filling the lower chamber taking what precious time she had away forever.

Her diagnosis with breast cancer filled everyone we knew with a sense of despair. I was struggling to make sense of it all with life's irony and the unexpected arrival of cancer into my life when these dreams started. I think the Merlin Dream was the way my mind reacted to this encounter with the life and death battles of these two women. That was the way of the Merlin Dream…to learn a great lesson from life.

In this state of mind, sleep entered my bedroom like a rare visitor. I was a pilgrim spirit in the Nether regions called insomnia. When sleep finally dropped its quiet curtain upon me, it would lead me into many strange encounters. Usually Merlin waited on the other side of this curtain of sleep...in the place of dreams.

One morning, after a busy night at work, I returned home exhausted. My wife had gone on to her workplace and I was home by myself. As tired as I felt, I could not relax. When I entered the bedroom, it was bright with the morning's sun so I deliberately pulled down the shades to darken the room. I stretched out on the bed and tried to sleep. Lying there in the enclosed room filled with dead summer air, I observed the white-sprayed nodules on the ceiling above me in the preternaturally darkened bedroom. I listened while the wind's hollow footsteps followed the angled patterns created by the eves of the building, screaming as it leapt off. I watched a single beam of light catch the amorphous dust in its eye as the sun pierced through a tear in the drawn shades. As I listened, I heard the incongruous sound of a dog barking in the distance. The sounds were twisted and distorted by the wind. I tried turning one way in bed and then tried the other. It seemed that sleep evaded me no matter what I attempted. Finally, for no reason whatsoever, sleep found me and drove me hard into that haunted land where troubled dreams are found.

Within the dream, I imagined myself lying on the ground enveloped by a thick blue fog, deep enough to cover me like a blanket. Something in this place disturbed me, even on this side of the wall of sleep. I pushed against the cool ground bringing myself to a sitting position where I had laid. I stood up and looked around while the dog-mists played wistfully about my feet and legs. It was night and something was moving fast through the distance beneath this cloudy mantel. I could sense it progressing doggedly in my direction. Away in the gloomy distance, the fog rolled back from the approaching object as it traversed its course along the murky ground. Still the turbid mists would not relent enough to unveil its true nature or form. I was not frightened by this phenomenon so much as I was curious about its peculiar activity. Transfixed, I merely continued to stand in the coiling tendrils and waited until the form either presented itself before me or passed me by. Just when my senses brought me to a realization that I should be a little afraid, the thick misty air parted, revealing what it had concealed. There suspended on the fog's leading edge, a wizard stood dressed in flowing black velvet robes.

His garments were decorated with golden symbols of stars, planets, and the moon in its many phases. On his head stood a pointed black hat rimed with golden bands and ornamented with old Runic symbols. His left hand held an old walking stick fashioned from a sapling he might have found in the forest. Fastened to his right side was a sword unlike any other I had ever seen. It was made entirely of clear crystal ending in a golden hilt bejeweled by a blue fire crystal atop its handle. Indeed the colored hues of fog were merely the resonance of this very blue light. The scabbard was nothing more than a golden ring through which the crystal blade slipped into and out of exposing the entire shaft of the blade to anyone who might see it. The wizard's name was Merlin. He never told me this…I just knew it instinctively.

Not really looking at me he asked, "Do you believe in the Once and Future King?" Then with a slow turn of the head, he looked me straight in the eye. He captivated me with his cold blue eyes while red-orange fires flashed in his pupils.

I hesitated before I answered him. I wondered what his question had to do with me. Why did he ask me this? I cautiously answered him, "Are you asking about King Arthur... the King Arthur who legends claim to have been the greatest king that ever lived?"

He raised his head, tilting back his pointed black hat. His hair was long and dazzling white. It appeared filled with red and white-hot sparks that never seemed to extinguish. His free hand moved freely toward his beard to stroke the wizened locks as he watched me suspiciously. Momentarily, it seemed as if he was going to answer my question. Suddenly he jerked his face away from me, as if something behind the twisted woodland brush startled him. Then with dramatic flair, he turned back to me just as quickly and stared at me.

He said not a word but started taking a visual account of my bare feet, worn clothes, and uncovered head. He appeared to be sizing me up like an undertaker estimating the dimensions of a coffin that will be imminently needed. My nerves began to get the better of me as I watched him continue this visual summary. My thoughts regarding this unwelcome examination were that he was simply unimpressed and was almost ready to dismiss me. I felt he was about to impart some type of unfair judgement about me based on how I appeared to him. Instead of being afraid of him, I became intensely angry. I became angrier than I had ever been in my life. Inside I felt the hot blood twisting in my veins as it began rising in revolt. He must have observed, or sensed, the anger mounting in the pit of my stomach. Without warning, he stopped his inspection and again concentrated on me by staring straight into my eyes.

He spoke slowly and carefully, watching my face for any interpretations that might be borne by the expression of my inner emotions… "A man must first know change before he can survive… Do you believe this?"

He was Merlin and I knew at once that he was looking for something special…perhaps someone to go on a quest…some adventure. As vengefully angry as I had become in those few moments before he spoke, I found it strangely effortless to release my anger as rapidly. I was eager to find out what he was searching for. After I was able to release a deep sigh, displacing the last vestiges of my anger, I responded almost defiantly, "Yes, I believe that it is so."

"Then you must change to survive," he said quietly, almost reverently. I continued to wonder what he was after so I listened as he continued speaking in these somber tones. "To do this," he paused and after taking a few steps toward an old tree stump continued, "you must survive change then you can truly live. Do you think you can do this and survive?" as he sighed deeply and turned to face me.

The question seemed so much like a riddle. But then, this was Merlin, a wizard who illustrated life's mysteries with magic and taught much about the world we live in with riddles. I didn't really understand what he had intended for me. I felt this was a dream and believed that in this dream nothing could hurt me no matter what Merlin had in store for me. Since I believed I was not in danger, I answered him, "Yes, I believe I can survive."

Merlin raised his staff above his head and suddenly the fog moved around us with slithering serpent-like coils made of blue ethereal smoke. I watched Merlin's mysterious gestures while he spoke his strange enchanted words. After losing my thoughts in his strange words, mesmerized by the blue swirling fog, I observed the full moon shining in the night sky. Eventually, like drowning in an ocean, collapsing in the incessant waves, the moon slowly disappeared within the entrails of the roving cerulean mists. The blue fog enveloped the surrounding naked trees, abandoned mossy rocks, and dead brown leaves blowing at my feet. Then, in a clear loud voice, Merlin spoke,

"Survive to Change
Change to survive...
In order to Live...
You must survive Change...
For Now,
You must
Change..."

Suddenly, I felt strange. The blue fog twisted and Merlin changed from a man into a large blue owl with harsh emerald eyes. The fog swirled like a whirlwind and through the funnel, I again saw the glow of the moon like a white reflection in a circular blue pool. When everything stopped it was the night of a full moon much earlier in my life. Merlin was gone, disappearing like the blue fog that had enveloped this same full moon not so long ago. In this new reality, I was a child again with my parents sleeping in a room next to me. Somehow, Merlin sent me back in time and was making me live my life all over again. I wondered, as I watched the clouds floating in the translucent glow of the moon, how different things could be…this time. Only I didn't realize what it was going to be like living it all over again…this time.

I had barely recovered my sensibilities when my mother walked into the living room some time in the early morning. I don't remember how I traveled to the living room from the bedroom. My last memory had been the full moon shining through the bedroom windows, but somehow that small trickery didn't matter anymore. The woman now standing before me was the same woman I always knew to be my mother, but she was definitely much younger than when I last saw her. She wore a cloth apron covered in red and white checks. She looked at me and said, "What are you staring at?" She laughed and shook her head at me. I suddenly realized Merlin changed me into a six-year old child sitting in the middle of a large throw rug covering the naked hardwood floor of our old living room. Nearby, I heard the sounds of my father shaving in our old bathroom where he left the water running in the sink like he always did. Old sounds, familiar sounds, sounds of my past young life comforted me while it surrounded me on all sides. It made me feel at home. It made me drop all the shields, walls, and barriers I built while growing up. I felt like I did when I was a child. My defenses were down. I was alive in a world of love, joy, and innocence. I felt as if I had really come home.

These feelings abruptly ended once I realized I had changed again. Only now, I had changed into the size and shape of a mouse, sitting in the middle of the throw rug. When my mother came looking for me and saw me as a mouse, she screamed for my father. My father hurried into the room as the residual vestiges of his human form melted into the quarrelsome guise of a large, gray tabby cat. Fearing for my life, I bolted under the sofa as my mother's screams trailed into the howl of an angry wolf. The sofa soon converted itself into a damp stone cave, as I transfigured into a creature with wings…a bat. At my father lunged at me in the form of a cat he metamorphosed into a hawk and my mother jumped as a wolf into the form of a sparrow. And so it went, we all became, at any given time, the predator, the prey, the covey, the brood, the family, the victims, the victors, the horror, the beauty, the heaven, the hell, the whole strange parade of life. While we were transfixed in this tumultuous process of transformation, I continued to grow in wisdom and stature through childhood, adolescence, and finally, my adulthood, until I grew to the age I am now.

The beginning of the dream always remained the same. Merlin came into my dream state and asked if I could survive change. When I told him I could, he changed me into a diversity of creatures that dwell upon this earth. With a perverse twist that only Merlin could perform, he also changed everyone I knew and loved into various strange animals, insect, birds, and reptiles. At any point in the dream, I could be a predator, a victim waiting to be slaughtered, or a spectator merely watching the various portraits of life being painted before me. He forced me to observe and participate in the many phases of my life, which he surrounded with his poetic and magical devices. He made me live through it all over again before he stopped the creative changes he designed not only for me, but also for the people I knew and grew up with as well. As I fell, triumphed, won, and lost, I relearned all those life lessons again as I not only progressed from a child to an adult but from an insect to an eagle.

When I had journeyed through the last of the changes, I found myself alone a mere few feet from the edge of a precipice. Beyond me, a panorama of dark jagged mountains encircled the cliff. In the place where I stood, a spiraling blue fog dressed my bare feet like ghostly shoes. Like a living entity, its tendrils were lacing and unlacing as I stood up riveted by the spectacular sight of razor-backed blue-violet mountains. I knew the ordeal had concluded but the dream had not. As expected, above a distant mountain, a cloud was bursting with red-orange white lightening, exploding dramatically. I knew Merlin was coming to send me back to the Land of Waking. In the guise of a great owl, he flew from the belly of the cloud to reappear at the very edge of this rock-strewn plateau in his human form.

He was the same wizard dressed in the same black velvet robes. However different strange designs embroidered the clothing with gold, silver, and sparkling gems. On his head was the appropriate pointed black hat complete with appliques to match the robes. He raised his head, tilting the pointed hat behind him. His hair was as dazzling white as it was before. His free hand moved to his beard to stroke the wizened locks as he eyed me warily. The place bathed in blue light captured the sharpened stone edges like reflections of glowing cold embers. The fog eddied at our feet in pools of blue then spilled away like running water off the edges of the blackened edges of rock. As always, inside the golden ring by his side, was the source of the bluish light. The blue gem within the hilt of the sword glowed in everlasting brilliance.

When Merlin transfigured from the shape of the owl to his present state, I managed to crawl to a flat black rock where I could rest. The many changes and metamorphoses Merlin had piled upon me left me exhausted. I knew his work was not yet complete. He had a great lesson, a revelation, only he would reveal to me when the moment was right. Although I kept saying to myself, "This is only a dream and dreams cannot harm you," I knew if the impulses were right, I could possibly die or end up paralyzed by a stroke while I was sleeping. After all, my physical body was exhausted from the many nights of insomnia. Who knew, at this quiet hour, what my heart was doing or how high my blood pressure might be? I knew I was alone in the house. My son was at school and my wife was at work. Neither one was expected back for several hours. I wondered what Merlin could do in this Dream World that would manifest itself in real physical harm in the Waking World. I realized, at this moment, that I could not wake myself in spite of the sheer terror this situation presented. Merlin truly had me under his influence! Everything I did and said from this time was an indication of whether I would wake from this dream or enter the realm of Endless Dreams.

For some space of time, he merely stared into another direction away from me. He peered beyond the edge of the precipice as if watching a distant vision floating over those desolate mountain peaks. Finally, he turned to me and spoke. "You have survived change," he said. Under the circumstances, it sounded more like a statement than a question.

His remark seemed to require a response so I nervously made a decision to speak. From a place deep inside, where courage is kept, I answered, "Yes, I have survived change."

This was Merlin and I knew my answers had a tremendous effect on the outcome of this journey. I felt, more than knew, he had the power of summoning up demons to carry me off to a cardiac arrest. With a word, he could possibly remove me from this reality altogether, abandoning me in an oblivion of paralysis or death. I knew my answers had to be correct. In a strange way, I desperately realized I might be in a position of real jeopardy.

He turned his back to me, then with only his head turned over his shoulder, he asked, "And what have you learned…" He unfolded his hands and raised them, giving the appearance of roots growing into the night sky. When he completely turned to face me, his hands were still outstretched as if he was performing a Benediction. He slowly finished his question,"…from all this?" His eyes looked first to the stars in the night sky then abruptly stopped and froze me with a stare from his cold pale-blue eyes.

I had to choose my answer carefully. What was most obvious? I was sure the first thing that entered my consciousness would be the answer he wanted to hear. I counted on my instincts to create the answer and finally spoke. "I learned that I could live through any change and survive."

As soon as my answer coursed the night air to the distance of his ears, he exploded in a fit of rage. "NO, NO, NO," he screamed into the misty night air, spinning around with each syllable. He raised his hands into fists, shaking them into the air above him. With each rotation he made in my direction, he would shake his fists, passing within inches of my face. Inside I felt my heart rate double and a hellish pressure built inside my head like the most intense migraine I had ever experienced. I was very afraid. I was not sure if my dream body was feeling this way, or if my real body was going through this as well. Merlin screamed insultingly into my face, "Is that all you have learned you stupid bog? Haven't I taught you anything?" Again he fixed me with his cold stare, but now his eyes blazed with molten anger. I knew he would expect a better answer with my next response. I had this one chance to come up with an answer before Merlin would make something happen. Already my heart trip-hammered so fast I could barely breathe. My chest was starting to ache from the exertion. Again, I couldn't be sure if this was happening in my dream body or really happening in my physical body. "What have you learned, Newt?", Merlin asked with as much contemptuousness as he could muster.

Only now did I realize that Merlin did not want me to look at this experience with my instincts. What he wanted from me was to look at this experience with my heart. Though it was my instincts that got me through the many metamorphoses he created, it was my heart he was trying to reach. I closed my eyes for a moment and began thinking about the many strange experiences I had seen. I remembered my father being changed into a housecat while I was changed into a mouse. Though it was the instinct of the cat to devour the mouse, the cat did not kill the mouse when it had the mouse trapped. When my father changed into an eagle and I was a sparrow, the eagle did not kill the sparrow but instead carried it high to a mountain and left it go free. My father had done this when I was leaving home for the first time. I thought of it as a very special gift to be shown the top of the world and then be allowed to fly into it from that vantage point. I thought it might have been every father's dream to be able to give his children that opportunity.

Once Merlin changed me into a fly. I was flying around when a sparrow became annoyed and began to chase me. The sparrow was actually my father at the time, I could only think as a fly and I did all I could to escape that sharp beak. I circled, dove, and finally flew into the crook of a tree. The sparrow flew off but I found myself entangled in a spider's web. I saw the spider coming as I tried in vain to free myself from the sticky web. I saw the spider's deadly jaws closing in on me. The spider gently removed me from the web and let me go. The spider was my mother. She was setting her son free from the safety of the web or the home in which I had grown comfortable. I felt it was at a time iny life when I was to move on into my adulthood. I remembered meeting my wife as a paired set of rabbits and setting up a house by building a nest as a pair of birds in a tree. I remembered watching my son as a foal newly born on dew scented grass and saw him following his mother as a clumsy young duckling behind a beautiful white swan. I remembered all the experiences that Merlin put me through and wondered about their meanings.

As I remembered them, I realized the people they represented were aware of who they were and what they meant to me and to each other. In spite of the animal instincts that Merlin created in them that should have set them to destroy one another, they had not. When Merlin sent his changes to make us the predator, the prey, the continuously amazing sphere of life, we still knew who we were deep down inside of us. No matter what happened to make us different on the outside, we were still the same basic stuff inside. There was something that existed deep inside us that kept us from destroying each other. We remembered that we were all possessed by something greater than the shells in which we found ourselves.

Finally, I realized what Merlin was after. In my haste to deal with my wife's diagnosis of breast cancer, I missed the most important of all truths to aid in my own self-healing. Though my wife had successfully dealt with her own healing, I had not. I believed I was the healthy one and I was impervious to anything that might harm me. I also felt guilty about not being able to carry some of the burdens the cancer experience dealt her. I had tried. I think I did all I could for her but what I could not do was lift the weight of the cancer burden from her and carry it for her like I wanted to. We all have our burdens to carry. And very much like a cat is destined to be a cat, and a bird is destined to be a bird, the person diagnosed with cancer must carry the burden themselves, no matter how much a person without cancer would like to carry it for them. You cannot turn a cat into a mouse and you cannot turn a bird into a fish. You cannot take the cancer upon yourself so the person affected is no longer affected. It just cannot be done. Not unless you are Merlin…and I am not. However just like the dream, the human spirit does change. We have a spirit that is a part of us that changes with the experiences we offer it and it grows and knows other spirits that are akin to it. We are all spirits here. No matter what happens to change us on the outside, no matter whether we are male or female, sick or well, no matter what color, nationality, whatever, we are all spirits. When you realize this, you begin to appreciate what it is that you are given and what is given to everyone. You begin to appreciate life in seconds, not years. You begin to appreciate a drop of water and are awed by an ocean. Merlin had shown me this. I was finally able to answer him. When I opened my eyes and finally looked into Merlin's angry face, I said, "I have learned that we are all spirits here."

His eyes softened as he became more human in his appearance. "Yes," he said, almost surprised by my response, "That's it." He stepped down from a high flat stone and walked towards me. As he moved he withdrew the crystal sword from the gold ring scabbard using his left hand then clasped it with the right. He raised the blade above him, and at a glance, gave the appearance he would strike, severing my head. Instead he bade me kneel before him and in strange phrases anointed me as if I were a knight. Afterward he asked, "Do you believe in the Once and Future King?" I was puzzled. I thought, "What a strange question to ask after putting me through all this." I really did not know how to answer him since I had vainly tried to answer him at the beginning of this dream. Of course, in the beginning, I had to ask why he was asking this question to begin with. Even then, he hadn't seemed to hear my response. Out of exasperation, I thought I would try to answer him. As I tried to speak, he placed a finger over my mouth, as a teacher would do to tell you to be quiet. He then turned away and with a whisk of his cloak, transformed into a great blue owl holding the crystal sword with the glowing blue stone in his talons. I watched him as he took flight, flying into the night sky, with the swirling blue fog enveloping him until I could no longer see him.

I rose from the stone precipice and watched as the fog receded from the sanctuary of rocks and disappeared somewhere beyond the confines of this rocky cliff. The sun glowed as a penumbra over the jagged edges of the far off mountain ridges. Finally, the skies parted their clouded horizons as I woke from this dream. I looked at the clock standing watch on the table near the bed and realized all this had taken only two hours to complete. I felt as exhausted as I did before lying down to sleep. The dream left me momentarily confused as I tried to collect my thoughts. I sat up on the side of the bed puzzling over the final question Merlin had posed to me… "Do you believe in the Once and Future King?"

The more I pondered the question the more convinced I became that it was just a silly dream. "Come on," I'd say to myself, "it was just a dream. It doesn't mean anything. You are letting it get to you by trying to validate it. Let it go." For awhile I seemed to be able to do just that, but somehow the question would eventually return to my thoughts like a cruel obsession. Sometimes I would hash it over in my thoughts for a time, and then I would later dismiss it, thinking it was silly to keep thinking about it. Repeatedly though, my dreams of Merlin would surface and Merlin would make me relive parts of the Merlin Dream again. Each time the dream would end with Merlin asking that same haunting question. "Do you believe in the Once and Future King?"

The dream was an annoying part of my life for a very long time. Eventually , the Merlin of my dreams faded like the Merlin of the old Arthurian legends. As with the legends of King Arthur, Merlin was lost in the Crystal Caverns of sleep caught in the spell of Nymuwe only to appear occasionally in the realm of dreams. Merlin's appearance in my dreams became less frequent as I felt his tenacious hold on me failing as my sleep patterns reestablished themselves.

One day, some months later, as I was cleaning off a shelf in my son's bedroom, I came upon a book we bought for him one Christmas. The book was about the historical King Arthur contrasted and compared with the legendary King Arthur. I wasn't thinking about Merlin's question at the time when I started reading several passages in the book. I remembered my love of reading about the Knights of the Round Table, the many feasts after a hunt, and the legends of Guinivere and Lancelot. I thought I would take a few moments to reacquaint myself with a book I had so loved as a child. As I read, I realized that at the time King Arthur existed, he had delivered the world out of a Dark Age and into one of enlightenment. He had made things better for his times. He forged a new era for the world, that was so intense and wonderful, that even for the brief moment it existed, it stood for all time and all times. It was the embodiment of all that is good and pure in this world.

Suddenly, in this waking epiphany, it all came rushing back to me! The Merlin Dream… I could almost feel the hairs rise on the backs of my arms. Merlin's question was not a question but a quest he had sent me on. He knew what I most wanted and had sent me into my world to find those answers that could help me find peace. At the time, I hadn't realized what he was asking. Only now, did I finally realize the significance of the question he had posed to me. "Do you believe in the Once and Future King?"

When Merlin had asked his question, he finished by placing his finger over my lips preventing me from answering him. At the time, I really did not understand what he wanted from me. I thought all he wanted was to impart some sort of insignificant information that would mean nothing to me. Now I knew the Merlin Dream was much more than understanding the spiritual aspect of our human natures, it was about hope. Merlin wanted me to believe in hope.

When I thought back to the time my wife was diagnosed with breast cancer I remembered thinking, "What will tomorrow bring?"

My tomorrow's were filled with the prospects of losing my wife, my son losing his mother, my wife's parents losing their daughter, my parents losing their daughter-in-law, and everyone's tomorrows looking very bleak. My wife, of course, had everything to lose and everyone. That lonely experience of losing it all must be a terrible place to find yourself in. This was the place she had been. Sometimes you have to hold hands in the dark before you can see the light. Sometimes you have to hold onto hope and believe the other person won't let go before you can pull them back from the specter of death.

I was there when my wife received chemotherapy. I was there when she had radiation treatments and physical therapy treatments to help return her arm to some type of functioning. I stayed with her when she was sick with nausea and vomiting after her chemotherapy treatments. I traveled with her on her trips to the hospital. I followed her to clinics on how to cope with cancer, scheduled lab tests with her, watched her while her lab values went up and down, prayed with her over bone scans, and made sure she made it to x-rays, mammograms, and the ever unfolding cancer story as it existed then. It was tough! No one should ever tell you the experience is easy to overcome unless they have been through it themselves. I've heard stories on occasion that breast cancer is not a disabling disease. I have listened as these same people proclaim breast cancer is easily defeated using the conventional therapies available. Perhaps the people who proclaim this diatribe should come and speak with the women who have gone through this. I believe their perception of how easy it is to survive breast cancer will change dramatically. Many women needing a mastectomy to save their lives never recover the full functioning of the affected side's arm. Some never have a day go by without their arm swelling to twice its size. Unfortunately, some give up rather than fight the battle every day for the rest of their lives. Still there are those who do not believe this is a disability. These same people even choose to look the other way.

All I am saying is, a cancer diagnosis changes the way a person looks at things. Perhaps, as in the more radical cases, cancer causes real physical changes too. Once cancer has entered your life, it is a trespassing thief robbing you of the sanctity of your home. Life is never the same for the cancer survivor or for the people who are close to that person.

Merlin's lesson was simple. Before the word "cancer" became part of my life, I had been living life without any "real" troubles.

Certainly, life had its problems, but overall, life was treating me well. When cancer entered my life unannounced, it removed all the control I had over my life and made me very angry. I responded in fear and contempt for the disease. I worked with my wife, the surgeon, the oncologists, and anyone who would help my wife conquer the physical conflicts with cancer. However, it was not as easy or as obvious to conquer my inner fears and precipitating anger with what the disease had done to her and our family.

Today, her cancer has succumbed to the treatments and now resides in the shadows of our lives. Undoubtedly, it could return one day for another fight, another conflict. Perhaps we will win again…perhaps not. Whatever the future holds for us, that battle is still in the future, in the darkening distance.

Merlin wanted me to find some closure with this disease. He wanted me to discover that it was alright to move on and live life to its fullest, to not feel afraid or guilty about living. Could things be as good as they were before the diagnosis of breast cancer? Only I could answer that. I was the one who had the instruments to make a life for the ones I most loved. So Merlin's question, "Do you believe in the Once and Future King?" was not about King Arthur at all. It was about discovering hope and serenity in my life again. Did I believe life would get better after this? Or, did I feel our lives had changed so dramatically that future chapters of our lives held less vitality and passion than before cancer entered our lives?

Sometimes I wish Merlin were here again. If he were, I would tell him that breast cancer has brought forth many great and shining moments for us. My son has also grown into a wonderful young man through this experience. I have grown through despair, anger, fear, acceptance, and now I believe the future is filled with hope and great challenges. Do I believe in the Once and Future King? Yes…for as long as there are heroes, warriors, and poets engaged in the war against breast cancer I believe there is hope for us all. We are all spirits here and when we have used up our space of life, we should be able to look back and say…we have done well.

Do you believe in the Once and Future King? Perhaps Merlin may find you in your dreams some day and you will have to try to answer him. What will you say?

Merlin (The Blue Dream)

As the story, "The Merlin Dream" states, Merlin was always surrounded by a blue fog every time he appeared in my dreams. I never have realized the significance of the blue fog, but I believe it was my psyche's attempt to keep me away from complete loss of sanity. The blue fog may have simply been a dramatic deception of reality as well. Either way, I have never been able to figure out the meaning of the blue fog other than it was a ominous and vigilant entity every time Merlin appeared. As the dream always seemed ghostly and frightening I incorporated ghostly, shadowy colors to create the receding forest and rushing fog stream. I used a black background for drama and to illustrate a kind of mystery in the drawing.

Drawing by,
George S. J. Anderson   1998-1999

The Setting of Autumn's Sun

"It was a time of reverence, a time for remembering, and a time for hoping."

"...there is a certain day in October that I promised myself I would not forget."

1996 George S. J. Anderson

Introduction

In the summer of 1996, I was given the opportunity to contribute a ten-inch by ten-inch square to a patchwork known as "The Skin Deep Exhibit, Stories In the Fight Against Breast Cancer," a project sponsored by the American Cancer society. I was trying to come up with an idea for several weeks without success. One day, I was reading an article in our local newspaper about someone getting a dozen roses when I realized what I would do.

Cancer seems to possess the power to take the sense of identity from each person, the sense of belonging to the human race. When my wife realized the grave implications of her breast cancer, she was afraid life had gone by without having contributed something that would be remembered in her name. She once told me, "I don't want to be forgotten." I didn't know if her remark stemmed from instinct or from frustration with the disease, but I knew I had to make her feel she would be remembered, especially if the cancer treatments were ineffective.

As the first anniversary of her diagnosis grew closer, I realized there should be a kind of celebration for this renewal of life. The anniversary of her diagnosis marked a great event for her. To my knowledge, there weren't any cards, ideas, or anything by which to celebrate this wonderful time. I was mulling around with an idea to help celebrate this special occasion when I read a newspaper article about someone receiving a dozen red roses for their accomplishments. A spark of inspiration elicited from that seemingly inane newspaper article moved me to act. I finally came up with something to celebrate her first special October evening. Some years later, when I was asked to put together a ten-inch square for "The Skin Deep Exhibit" I saw a second article about roses in our paper which brought back memories of that first October evening. After that small memory jog, I eventually went to work and wrote down the story that grew out of those experiences. Each year I continue this celebration of life on the

anniversary of her diagnosis. I call the story "Twelve Roses."
    That first October evening, in the setting of the autumn's sun, something wonderful happened.

Portrait of the Universe

There were days I could have laughed…
But didn't
There were days I could have cried…
But couldn't
There were days I should have said…
But passed them by
Then there were years that were…
But then they lost their time
There were tears that should have fallen…
But eyes were too dry…
Then there were days of vision…
But no one could see…
And all I could do was
Take my brush
And with my single color
Paint the world
Hoping to add to
That portrait of the universe
The color it might be missing
If not touched by
My hands

1978 George S. J. Anderson

Twelve Roses

Each year on a day in October, I go to a flower shop and buy my wife a dozen roses. It is not her birthday, or our anniversary, and it's not because I forgot to do something. It is the day we were told she had breast cancer. That day lives in my mind as a nightmare of lost hope, mortal despair, and holding hands in the dark. Besides dealing with our own fears of cancer, we needed to go home and tell our twelve-year-old son the same bad news.

Several years have passed since that ill-fated day when I heard, "Your wife has breast cancer." Those words still ring in my memory like a cold hollow bell sending chills up my arms and down the nape of my neck when I think about it too long. I remember her saying, because of her fears of dying, "I don't want to be forgotten." I watched her as tears struggled at the corners of her eyes. She was trying to be brave and was not quite willing to let them roll down her cheeks. I remember the struggle she went through to hold on to this fragile life. She fought this disease with the tenacity of a fighter, a survivor. She has that special kind of heroism shown only to those who watch and wait. I was there for her. I will always be there.

Now each year I buy her a dozen roses in October. My son is aware of these proceedings and playfully criticizes; "You're not doing that again, are you Dad?" I explain, "This is an important day in your mother's life." I tell him that for each year his mother survives I add one pink rose to replace one white rose to complete the full dozen. "Then why not just buy the pink roses?" he asked. "I buy the white roses because they are like uncolored canvases, they are the hope and the promise that each year your mom will survive and receive another pink rose in the dozen." Gesturing for him to hand me the gardener's shears I added, "I think your mom looks forward to this, don't you?" "Well," he said as he watched me cut the stems, "I guess so."

For a while we both stood there as father and son. He handed me the long-stemmed roses. I made wedge-shaped cuts on them while he arranged them in the vase as I returned them to him. It was a time of reverence, a time for remembering, and a time for hoping. When we stepped back and admired the roses he asked, "What happens when all twelve roses are pink?" I thought for a moment of what he was asking me then said, "I guess I will just have to buy twelve more…twelve more roses with a pink one for every year she survives." Then he asked rather gleefully, thinking I had left something out, "Why did you pick twelve as the number of roses you would give her?" I never did tell him the answer to that one, but there is a certain day in October that I promised myself I would not forget…

Twelve Roses

Twelve Roses was drawn to typify a normal but abnormal occurrence during the period of chemotherapy with cancer treatment. In this drawing, you will see the white form for the wig sitting at the table with a string of pearls and the hairpiece. The vase of roses sitting on the table, of course, is reminiscent of the story the drawing is named after. The setting of natural elements (the roses and the pearls) is at odds with the unnatural ones (the wig and the wig form). I used many shades of red in the background to exemplify the conflicts expressed in the foreground.

Drawn by George S.J. Anderson, 2000

Coming Full Circle...Winter's Doorway Revisited

"It is the responsibility of the existing generation to teach the one after how to reach greater goals and resolve those questions the generation before it could not."

"From the moment of our birth to the moment of our death we are given a space of time to show the worth of our being here."

1997-1998 George S. J. Anderson

Introduction

1992 was the year I received the news of my wife's breast cancer. Earlier that year, I was preparing my son for his first hunting experience, which would take place in the fall. He had grown to the magical age of twelve that year. We both eagerly anticipated our upcoming hunting adventures together with the passing summer months and the approach of the cooler weather that precedes the autumn season. As all new hunters are aware, you need a hunter's safety course in order to get a hunting license. Since the ruling was not in effect when I became a new hunter, I had never taken a hunter's safety course. So to make amends for myself and to make him more comfortable with the course, I decided to join him. I spent most of the summer preparing beside him for the upcoming hunting season. When my wife discovered she had breast cancer in early autumn, it quickly put this part of our lives on hold.

The course of breast cancer treatments followed the diagnosis, our days built into weeks, our weeks into months, and my time to hunt with my son in the autumn of that year slipped silently away. By some small fortune, my father was able to take my son hunting on a few rare occasions they both had a chance to go. Another year passed without any possibility of taking my son on a hunting trip. Finally, after two years had gone by, I had the chance to take him deer hunting. I was fortunate to have had the opportunity to hunt with my son this one time. It was an experience for us both.

One of the sad facts I realized as I went hunting with him that year, was how quickly our time together was passing. A mere two years had passed between that eager twelve-year old without a care in the world till now. Now, of course, breast cancer had entered both our lives in very subtle ways that even I was not quite willing to admit. It had placed a mark on both our lives that took pieces of life away from us and rarely ever gave them back. Time was one of those things that had slipped away from both of us. Still, we needed to make the most of our time as we had it to give to each other. I believe that may be the one thing cancer, in any form, gives back…to value the time we have together.

So it was, the year I traveled with my son to the mountains that I came full circle in my journey through the seasons of cancer. Just as I had gone to the mountains with my father on my first deer hunt, so my son came with me on his. I was not expecting anything out of the ordinary on this excursion, but as every hunt goes, something happens to make it unique. As the events of the day unfolded before us, it became a special time for both of us.

The Hour of the Child

Mother lay down your apron
Leave your pots on the stove
Let the world here that surrounds us
Sit on the windowsill with the rose
There is a breeze blowing a song around us
Filled with eloquent laughter of a child
He is a moment of an hour
A discordant note of song
Bejeweled with eyes of sapphire light
Aglow with the face of the sun
He plays games with twenty questions
And my answers always ten too few
He asks me of God and I tell him the sky
Is His window and the clouds are His beard
Now giving into a moment of sleep
We both watch as his hour slips away
Soon this child will be a man but for now
Let him dream his dreams
Beneath the blanket of sleep
On the wake of the apple-blossomed ground

1981 – George S. J. Anderson

Wolves in the Woods

In these mountain woodlands, you can take time and search for those things that are deepest inside you. Within the wind's capricious dance with the swaying branches of the naked trees you can listen to the whispering heart you never heard. In the silent shadows of the wooded timberlines you might find a child that lost you in the crying din and rampant rage of the dying sky. It is here you may listen to a litany of sounds singing softly within the shadows of foggy ravines and dark forests of the mountain terrain. Somewhere here you might find something you were never hunting for, and once you have found it you will never forget.

Two years passed since I hunted in these woods. It seemed I was here only a short while ago, before the words "breast cancer" entered my family's life. Somewhere before, in that guileless time, I hunted deer here. Those times have passed quickly and seemed in retrospect childishly carefree. I walked through these wooded places looking, hunting, and sensing where deer might have hidden the night before. Now, my intentions were different. I felt a lingering sense of ambivalence about getting a deer as the focus of my journey now leaned toward my son's hope to see one for his first time.

As I thought about bringing him to these mountains, the changing autumn leaves inspired a somber introspection within me. I found myself led back to a place where I once found peace in an otherwise bleak, tumultuous world. I was summoned by a deep inner voice that spoke in a language other than mere words. I didn't understand it yet, but something was to happen on this journey which would affect me for the rest of my life. At the time, it seemed too insignificant to commit to my memory, but now when I call it to mind, I believe it was the best life's lesson I ever learned.

After two years, I was bringing my son with me to hunt in the woods where at least three generations of my ancestors had hunted before me. It was a pilgrimage delayed by my wife's untimely diagnosis with breast cancer and her pressing need for cancer treatment. The year I was to bring him with me to the mountains he would have been twelve. Then, he would have been the same age I was when my father first brought me to hunt deer. Cancer caused that time to drift away from us. As he sadly realized, I exploited all my free time the previous year caring for his mother. Since then, time silently transformed my son into a young man of fourteen, eagerly awaiting his chance to hunt his first deer. I hoped the first deer hunting experience would be a special one for him. At the time, I did not realize the evolution we would go through on this journey.

Sometimes the mountain terrain can distort the things you see before you. At times, it is like a perfect illusion existing inside a strange reality. Sometimes, it is the atmosphere affecting what you believe you see, or perhaps like some illusion, it narrows your perceptions of what your sensibilities allow you to see. So it was on the day we ventured into the wilds to hunt deer. The relentless rain challenged our progress as we journeyed towards the mountains. Though it felt cold enough to snow, the rain persisted with freezing cold droplets that made our conditions seem much more adverse than what they actually were. Several hours from our home we arrived at the place where we were going to hunt. We left the pickup truck that brought us here parked near the top of the mountain a safe distance into the woods. The rain possessed a quality of penetrating coldness so, we decided to bring a blue plastic tarp along to repel the rain and prevent us from getting soaked to the bone on our stand.

Finally, when the time came for us to advance into the woods, we abandoned the comfortable confines of the truck and outfitted ourselves with rifles, thermoses, ponchos, and the large blue tarp. With all our parcels secured, we slowly ventured into the cold wet darkness of the mountains with hopes of getting a deer.

Stealthily we walked down one of the mountain paths hewn out of the woody vegetation. The trees and brush had readily relinquished their hold of colored leaves to the forest floor. The wet leaves did not betray our position with their whispered cracklings inherent to the forest floor during dry weather. Instead, they aided our progress in softened silence as we stepped over wet branches and fallen trees. My son, uncomfortable with our tormenting weather conditions, whispered softly to me several times, "Are we there...are we there yet?" I merely answered him,

"No, not yet," or simply, "I'll let you know."

In spite of all our diligent preparations, we were getting cold and wet. I knew the weather conditions were not going to let up for quite a while. I continued pushing through the wet scrub brush and dripping mountain laurel trying to find a place close to where we wanted to hunt. I agreed with my son protesting his uncomfortable state, I too was hoping to stop soon and make a stand to get out of the freezing, driving rain.

I was looking for one of those places that with a hunter's divination would allow us to see deer yet let us throw our tarp over something to stay dry. Finally, I found it. The place seemed to materialize near the top of the mountain. I looked below us and saw where the ground fell away at an abrupt grade. Still, it was not so steep that a deer in flight could not climb it. This was the area where we would stop and make a stand.

The chosen place had three large trees in a sauntering line with two fallen trees wedged tightly across all three. One tree had fallen into this array at waist level while the other was about five feet above it. When some of the smaller branches had been broken away, the natural fall of the higher limbs would make the tarp easy to fasten above us and keep the rain off. My son held our rifles while I set about the task of preparing our stand. I completed the whole setup in about twenty minutes. Soon we were standing comfortably in our makeshift stand with the rain drumming on the tarp over our heads. Occasionally, I would look up as water beads collected in rivulets and ran off the sky-blue edge of plastic in a steady stream. We had worn plastic ponchos over our clothing to keep us dry. After securing the tarp above our heads, we removed them so the crackling sounds of plastic did not interfere with our already sodden perceptions of sound.

When all our amenities were satisfied, and we were sure we would be able to maintain some silence, we did what we could to make ourselves comfortable. We stood with our rifles slung crosswise over our chests and braced our arms on the horizontal fall of the tree before us. This way we could stabilize our rifles if a buck happened to put in an appearance.

We listened and waited as the rain realized its lethargy and fell to a slow steady splash before it finally ceased altogether. Eventually, all we heard was the occasional dripping sound the rain-soaked branches made upon the makeshift tarp roof that stretched over the barren branches above us. When the aberrant sounds of the rain ceased, the woods shrouded itself in a quiet reverence like an empty sacristy. It was into this strange silence that my thoughts of the past, present, and future arrived like strangers trying to find seats in the confines of my thoughts. As I looked deeply into these silent woods, my son held vigilance over the dark forest of my ancestors. I withdrew into my silent realm while I secretly knew his hopes of seeing a deer remained harbored within his sanctuary of peaceful dreams.

As we waited in that cold humid environment, the air became noticeably colder. Before our eyes, the wet air slowly materialized into strange amorphous shapes. Some of it appeared as a spectral fog designed in misty layers of white. While I was watching, the mists began to grow whitened creepers, wrapping themselves like thick white vines around the soggy black bark that clothed the trees. The air before us developed ghosts, outlawed to the mountainsides, which descended in vertical, cylindrical, horizontal, and thick twisted forms. Eventually, the forms melted together, the shapes falling, some rolling, some pouring themselves away toward the depths of the mountain, like souls parading to some forgotten domain. Finally, they melted into one body succumbed by sleep, like a weary ghost falling into a cradle, near the bottoms of the mountain. However, every time the wind shifted position the ghostly mass rolled and moved like an enormous white wall.

We watched this strange weather phenomenon with interest as the whim of the wind caused the wall of mist to recede, leaving our visual perimeter very clear, or encompass us, leaving us almost blinded. The fog seemed to dampen the acuity of sounds in our perimeter as well. Distant sounds were muffled and distorted by its presence. We were unable to distinguish if they originated nearby or from some distant site on the mountain. I was always relieved when the fog passed us. It seemed to possess a surrealistic quality that made me uncomfortable when it surrounded me in its murky wet cloak. I sensed the same feeling emanate from my son as I watched him study the movements of the fog. As the morning progressed, we watched this wall of fog moving imperceptibly up and down the slopes. It was like an animate entity, moving from one side of the mountain to the other like a bowl of milk slowly tilted back and forth by unseen hands.

Above us, on the highest point of the ridge, I could hear squirrels jumping from the trees, landing in the wet scrub brush and wet leaves. Toward the lower side of the mountain, I heard the unmistakable sound of a mountain bobcat. My son also heard it and asked what "that sound" was. I heard this cry only once before in my lifetime. It stirred mixed feelings of happiness and sadness to hear it again.

I was thinking back on a day when I heard a bobcat cry for the first time. In my thoughts, I envisioned a time in my forgotten past when I was only thirteen or fourteen years old. It was one of the last times I had gone hunting with my grandfather. That day, my grandfather and I were walking through these same woods together. I remembered we were on our way to hunting ruffled grouse in the mountain bottoms. After we had walked through some thick underbrush in the direction to the bottoms, we happened upon a mountain bobcat sitting on an old rotting stump. Before I stumbled into it, my grandfather grabbed me by the shoulder and stopped me. We stood there briefly when the cat rounded at us. It growled, left out a scream, then exploded in a burst of speed, which could only be described as "a blink of an eye." The eerie sound of its screaming resonated through the mountain ravines and stayed with me ever since. My grandfather passed away only a year or two after this experience as I now remembered him saying, "Now, you won't ever forget the sound of a bobcat." As I listened in both the present and the past, I realized that I never had. Now, secreted somewhere within the wooded mountain ravines, that same sound resonated in an eerie scream hidden below our stand.

Mountain bobcats are shy creatures, and by nature, they remain unseen and silent in the mountainous terrain. They are not dangerous creatures generally, but chance encounters are unusual. In size, they seldom grow any larger than a good-sized housecat. However, when the cries mingled with the lonely solitude of the woods they became piercing, haunting, and resonating like terrible sounds of tormented spirits. During our brief encounter with the bobcat, the howls merged inside the strange mist and created a faux supernatural aura to our presence in the woods. Within my own psyche, I felt a strange penetrating sense of isolation. While listening to the unnaturally broken silence, we heard another shriek abrade the quiescent air from the opposite direction. I realized this abrupt change of direction meant two bobcats were prowling the area together. The sounds continued like mirrored shrieks echoing above and below the ridge where we stood. I told my son, "We are not the only hunters in the woods, these cats are stalking something." While I listened to the progression of their cries, it became apparent that the prey they were stalking was us.

Did something in their instincts make them hesitant to

investigate the prey they were stalking on the hill? Did they realize that they were stalking the most dangerous foe they could have encountered, men? At first, their futile wails resounded above and below our position. As I listened to their progress in the leaves and brush, I could hear one of them shift cautiously to the front of our stand while the other moved slowly behind us. The cats maintained the same distant perimeter, never venturing any closer than they were at that moment. The cats' recondite nature did not betray a single glimpse of them during their predatory performance as we waited for deer.

While this weird pursuit of the hunters and the hunted progressed, I listened to a strange snapping sound erupting over the forest treetops above us. As I viewed the immediate landscape and listened for the direction of the sounds, I watched a dark shape closing on us by way of the sky above our heads. I recognized the dark-winged creature, flying at tree level, as a wild turkey, perhaps fleeing the pursuit of some unknown predator of its own. I pointed this out to my son as he looked through the naked tree limbs into the sky above us and saw it himself. He seemed very annoyed by the turkey's noisy progress while it made its way over us. Eventually, the large gray-black bird flew away, again leaving the sanctity of the woods in relative silence. I listened for the bobcat's eerie cries to continue, but their presence seemed to have faded like those distant memories surfacing with thoughts of my grandfather.

A great distance away, a shot rang out, its report followed the contours of the ravine to our location. In its dying wake, another shot fired, but closer this time. I told my son to get ready. If deer were advancing in front of these shots, then they would definitely be moving towards us. Another shot rang out below us then another burst of fire exploded to our left as a slight breeze picked up and breathed heavily against our faces.

With the breeze blowing at us, I watched incredulously as the massive wall of thick white fog moved unchecked up the mountain slopes and surrounded us. It was almost as if a sinister intelligence controlled it. I was dumbfounded. Until now, the fog had receded, leaving us undisturbed, settling into the lower regions of the mountain ravines and lowlands. At the instant these thoughts began taking shape in my mind, the fog slipped below us again. It then settled like a great ghostly veil about a hundred yards below the ridge and stationed itself there. Its malign intelligence taunted us with its whitened caul. Almost magically, two deer materialized out of it. They moved like carved animated reliefs, appearing to walk off the misshapen misty wall into our sight. I pushed the safety off my rifle then told my son to be ready to fire if these deer had antlers.

The two deer stepped furtively in and out of the white mass before us. As if the deer sensed a presence watching them, they responded by melting into the outermost layers of mist provided by the sheer curtain of fog. The deer's fortunate encounter with our foggy ridge made it difficult to visualize them from our position. I whispered softly to my son to examine them for horns before he took a shot. I had an advantage visualizing the deer since my rifle had a scope. My son's rifle was not equipped this way, which made his observations of the deer more difficult. Eventually, the deer carelessly wandered in front of us and I saw the two deer were only does, not the buck we were hoping to see.

I rested my gun against my chest then reset the safety. I watched my son studiously observe the two deer while sighting down the barrel of his rifle. I thought, perhaps the fog was giving him some trouble, so I said, "I think they are just doe, but keep checking until you're sure." My son's intense observations made me feel that I hadn't examined the deer long enough and had missed seeing a set of horns. I asked him, "Do you see horns?" He broke his concentration for only a split second then resumed his stance as the deer moved slowly below us and up the slope toward our right.

Our position on the mountain slope gave the deer the appearance of large bodied creatures. The thick white fog entangling them further erased their long graceful legs, mysteriously concealed by the steep embankment. From some distant outpost, discordant remains of rifle fire penetrated the air. The atmosphere quickly saturated with an almost palpable sense of caution. As such, the two deer retained their stance by keeping their heads positioned parallel to the ground. Their course of escape from this deadly area was achieved using this deception.

I knew something was wrong when my son pulled back the hammer of his rifle. I did not know if the fog had blinded his perception or if the deer's deceptive stance provoked him, but I watched him remove the safety and prepared to fire. Again, I asked him, "Do you see horns?" I squinted my eyes trying to see what, I felt, had perhaps eluded me when I observed them earlier. No matter how I tried to visualize them, I could see nothing different; the deer were unquestionably doe, not bucks. I reached over and stopped him from firing his rifle.

I said, "Let the hammer fall back without firing." He did as he was told. Again, I asked him, thoroughly confused by his behavior, "Did you see horns?" He looked at me as strangely as I was speaking to him in a foreign language.

"Horns?!" he responded, as if I had asked him a confusing question.

"Yes. Horns....We are hunting deer, you know," I said, feeling very confused by the direction this conversation was going.

He twisted his head toward me while he elicited the most peculiar look on his face and said, "Dad! Wolves don't have horns!"

"Wolves?", I asked, thoroughly surprised and confused by his response. I was startled initially then thought about the way the deer had presented themselves on the mountain's ridge.

I told him, "These woods do not have any wolves in them... Why, on earth, would you think those deer were wolves?" It was then, when the moment had passed, that the whole confusing situation seemed amusing to me. I started to laugh, but after looking at him, I realized he was not as amused by the situation as I was. In fact, he actually seemed to be angry that he believed the two deer were wolves. The rise and fall of the land, the appearing and disappearing tendrils of fog, the feeling of isolation one feels in the mountain terrain, and the lack of experience of a novice hunter, had fooled him.

I thought about the illusion the deer created while they were passing before us on the foggy slope. The deer, clothed in their dark winter coats, appeared dark gray-brown rather than the rusty red-brown colors they wore during the summer and early fall. Our view of them was conclusively distorted by the stance the deer chose to avoid detection. My son, an inexperienced hunter, observed the distorted impressions of their bodies suspended in the mantle of mists. The deer maintained their positions at a linear stance rather than the upright position a deer would have normally taken. The surrealistic quality of the foggy terrain had deteriorated our visual field to such a point that when I put it all together I finally saw what my son had seen, "wolves in the woods." Still it was a contrivance of the mind, an illusion created by the mountain's peculiar weather conditions that presented this strange impression of wolves running along the ground in the mists.

I realized how he had been honestly tricked and frightened by the strange apparitions the deer had created before us. Without a doubt, my son had seen wolves. When he saw what his mind interpreted to be wolves, he did what he felt was necessary. He tried to protect us both. He told me later that day he was not going to shoot them unless they decided to turn back on us. It was only when the deer had made a sudden turn up the hill that he had pulled the hammer back and prepared to fire. When I thought he was about to fire on them, I stopped him. Afterwards, the deer, as expected, hurried away towards the bottom of the mountain disappearing into that silken white fog like a dream that never happened.

That day we learned something about each other and our fears. Memories of past times reminded me of old lessons learned as a boy. My son's journey began by looking for deer but ended by seeing wolves on his first hunt. Just decades ago, I went hunting in these ancient mountains and found the white deer. During our hunt, one of our ancestors appeared in my thoughts to remind me of the cries of the mountain bobcat. Through these memories, I imparted knowledge to my son, not fear. In a way, an ancestor spoke through me and explained something about the world to my son. It was through a man he never met, except in faded photographs, that he would now remember the sounds of the mountain bobcats.

We enjoyed the rest of our day in the mountains. Several times that day we changed the position of our stand in the mountains. We dismantled the tarp over our heads and tried hunting on the other side of the mountain later in the afternoon. Eventually, the sun made its way through the gray clouds while the wind swept the strange fog out of the mountain lowlands and into the memories of our past. We never saw any more deer that day but we did see "wolves in the woods."

Eventually we returned to our home and related the story of the "wolves in the woods" to our friends and relatives. They were all intrigued and amused by the circumstances of the story and were glad to have us back home. As all things grow to pass, the story faded into the scrapbook of our memories and eventually found a place in our forgotten pasts.

There are days when my thoughts return to those primitive mountains. Sometimes I try to imagine the way of life the native Indian tribes had when they flourished there in centuries past. They would call the experience my son had gone through as finding his "spirit guide." According to their ancient beliefs, when a young man came of age he would go into the world to find his "spirit guide." Usually the entity would come to the young man during some experience of enlightenment or hardship and would help him through it. This "spirit guide" would then stay with him for life and guide him through the difficult times in his life.

Our Indian ancestors held firm to sacred beliefs about chance encounters with their "spirit guides." When they came of age, the tribal elders sent the young men into the wild lands without food or water to search for these guardian spirits. They could not return to their homes until they transcended from the experience and had it validated by the elders in the tribe. The elders believed these experiences were a type of symbolic testament to our human natures. In the past, when I needed something to cling to, my memories of the white deer returned and helped me struggle through a very difficult time. My son will have a memory of two wolves moving freely through the misty forests which may gain some clarity for him as he journeys through his life. Again, the spiritual nature of the woods carved another perspective inside the deepest parts of me.   I glimpsed a renewed religious aspect of them as the experiences sent roots into the essence of my spirit.

In spite of the superficial understanding of what had happened on the mountain that day, I continued to have concerns about what my son believed. The wolves he saw were certainly not real wolves. Yet, when I spoke with him later about the wolves, I could tell he was not entirely convinced. I believe he saw them out of the eyes of fear, not with the eyes of clarity.   When I looked through my son's eyes for that instant, taking on the cloak of fear he wore, I truly saw it take the form of wolves. I knew how to explain the deer were not wolves but how would I help him release the fear that captured him? I realized his mother's cancer had affected him on a deeper level than he would ever be able to decipher for himself. It would take a long time to work through all the fears potentially created by watching his mother battle breast cancer. Had it affected him to such a point where he would envision fear in places where fear had no merit?

With parenting, we rarely observe the effects of the lessons we teach our children. Sometimes, our reaction to a given situation teaches a life's lesson, which may be intrinsically profound. Other times, it is the information we don't offer them that has the greater influence. It is our responsibility to teach our children about the things courage can overcome and sometimes, more importantly, what it cannot. We all hope our children have the ability to progress further than we have and follow their dreams in directions only they can follow. Thinking back on all the lessons my father taught me, I begin to realize I achieved a greater inner peace and find myself moving toward a greater realization of my potential than my father ever did. I believe it is the responsibility of the existing generation to teach the generation after how to reach greater goals than it did, and resolve those questions the generation before it could not. We should give our children aspirations to dream of better things, to show them life can be born out of ashes, and not to forget the past for what it can teach them about the future.

Sometimes, we need to teach a reasonable amount of fear to our children that will assure their survival. We need to say it is okay to climb to the top of a tree but we must also explain that it is not reasonable to jump from the top of it. This kind of fear is good fear. If you teach them to be afraid of climbing a tree then you have lessened the scope of what they might be willing to try in life. Perhaps a tree will not be the focus of something they try later, but symbolically, it may represent something overwhelming to them because of not trying (something) in the past. I was afraid of what happened to us when my wife's breast cancer was diagnosed several years ago. I remembered my own conflicts and resolutions as I searched for answers during my bouts with insomnia. I wondered if my son could not move on, could not try new and different things in his life, whether he was afraid to climb the tree again, or had he considered jumping from the top of it.

Our fears of breast cancer returning to our lives every day became exhausting and would not allow us to carry on with our normal activities of life. Living with a survivor of breast cancer and understanding it would not affect our lives this particular day and time was something each of us had to overcome in our own way. A legacy of survival and hope was what I wished to pass on to my son. Cancer was now like those "wolves in the woods" he saw that day, apparitions of reality with no substance of a threat. Nevertheless, cancer could strike again like a real wolf; it could be lying in wait, hidden, snarling, waiting for the right moment to strike out at us again. However, at this moment, it existed like the "wolves" my son saw that day, an illusion borne of fear and inexperience.

When breast cancer threatened my wife's life, I was holding my anger for so long it threatened to release itself in rage. I wanted to pick up a weapon of some kind and strike out at it. However, cancer is not an enemy you can physically strike. I existed with an abundance of pent-up rage with no where to place it. My wife did not deserve it, she was having enough trouble dealing with surgery, chemotherapy, radiation, and her fears of cancer. My son did not deserve it, he barely understood why everything in his young life was undergoing such turmoil. Finally, I turned the rage inward and from it came a flood of tears while driving home alone from work, a terrible haunting sadness, a growing insomnia, and these stories. When I started a support group for men who were partners of women diagnosed with breast cancer, I was intrigued by their familiar and similar experiences. There was a need for this kind of support. There was also a need for the support of the other family members of the woman diagnosed with breast cancer. Breast cancer is not just a woman's disease but a disease that affects whole families, including young children.

One day my twelve-year old son (at that time) came home and told me a story that showed the kind of heroism that I admire. I contacted my son's school when the diagnosis of breast cancer came up and explained what he was up against at home so a counselor would sit and talk with him. I called the school several times because I felt I had valid concerns regarding my son's ability to cope with his mother's illness and still do well in school. I wanted the school to be aware of any potential problems before they became insurmountable. Incredibly, every time I called his school I was told that the student would have to ask for help himself before they would do anything. Really, did they believe a twelve-year old would ask for help in anything, especially something this serious?

Since the adults at the school were unwilling to take the first step, my son was pretty much dealing with the diagnosis and treatment of his mother's breast cancer on his own. I told him one day that the best thing he could do for his mother was to work hard in school and get good grades. As you might well imagine, easier said than done. Even under these adverse circumstances, my son was able to achieve the highest grade in his science class that year. The day he discovered he had done so well, a thoughtless student said, "Well you can't say you have A's in all your subjects like I do." My son replied, "Well your mother doesn't have breast cancer like my mother does either." He told me the boy stopped taunting him after that. He also told me his friends gave him a pat on the back for his clever and honest reply. It was good to hear that he could speak openly with his friends and classmates. Ironically, the adults who were there to help him through this were deafeningly silent. In a sense, my son was dealing with "wolves in the woods" of another kind. These people were supposed to be there to offer support and care during a difficult time. Instead, they offered only silence and apathy.

The earth often feels like a cold and hungry place. We walk over this earth searching to satisfy our gnawing hunger of being alone. Although we are alone when we come into this world and we are alone when we depart from it, we cannot forget our short space of time here may make a significant impression on someone. From the moment of our birth to the moment of our death, we are given a space of time to show the worth of our being here. During our beginnings and endings, we will enjoy many meetings and partings, find brief joys, and know the warmth of others. The trick, if you call it that, is clinging to those brief moments of warmth and being with someone that will satisfy you enough to go onto the next phase of living, dying, or becoming. By filling our hollow bowls with these experiences we may sate our hunger and pass the bowl filled with these experiences to the generation after. I want to fill my bowl with life and hope, not fear, and pass it to my son.

Somewhere in the mountain timberlands, there is a place where the deer and the wolves exist together. As predator and prey, they learned to respect their relationship with each other. Each entity has understood its life and death struggles with each other and the eventuality that they all face some day. Therefore, while this passage of time exists for us we should understand how life needs to be experienced to its fullest. "Wolves in the woods" may come as an unwelcome reality to us all at some point in our lives. After all, the moment we are born we begin to die. It is what we have done with the time we have, that will count for something. While we can, do something amazing, teach the people around us, teach our children, and teach others how to live in the face of impossible odds. Pass on a legacy of hope. Sometimes you do get the chance to change things. Let those people you know and love be inspired by what you do and say so they, too, will want to make a difference with their lives.

In my many journeys through life, I try to capture and experience the great moments, triumphs, and beauty planted within a dream of scars. These special moments become important and as real as those deer roaming through the colors of a late autumn forest. While realizing these great moments, I reluctantly watch for the wolves in the woods, to be potentially aware of them. Somehow, I never remember them too long that I forget to live life to the fullest. After all, why would we survive only to fear the next day? Every day we have a chance to influence the life of someone special. Someone you don't know could be affected by your courage to survive, to live. In my eyes, my wife is a warrior and a hero. Her courage to survive has taught us life does come out of ashes. As for my son, I have watched him grow through adversity and saw many times when he showed me courage under fire. They are both heroes in different ways.

Several years have now passed since the deer hunt with my son. We continue to hunt together when we each find the time. Though those special times have fallen to the past, we still look forward to the new experiences still before us. Nevertheless, I doubt that either of us will ever forget the experience of the "wolves in the woods." At least, I never will.

For me, a moment arrives on the early winter air when I sense a distant voice emanate from the mountains. It is there that I sense restless sounds in the emerald green laurel and twisted brush of these Appalachian highlands. It is here I continue listening, hoping to hear something in the place where a boy grown to a man keeps his heart. I can't help believing in a place where a white deer stands listening to the rising wind, in a place where the wind rustles with sounds like prayers whispered on a wooded mountainside. Within those ancient mountains, I can still find a quiet calmness that soothes me. Perhaps the wind carries a certain kind of peace nestled within the touch of this early winter air. Sometimes, I need to find my way back and remember the lost pieces of my life. I need to feel the quiet solitude, then return to my life, renewed. In this late autumn reverie, I sit upon a stained rock surrounded by the quiet noise of autumn's dying leaves. Watching as each one descends to the ground, I am haunted by their sounds. I sit silently, listening to their voices speaking softly like whispers from a dream. I hold on to their memory…so many have fallen.

Wolves in the Woods

This drawing was created using dark conflicting colors, like the black against orange, and pink and purple in the darkening sky. Like the story by the same name, the concept was one of being ominous and hidden, like the shapes of the wolves half-hidden by the tall brush and broken sticks in the foreground. The concept of foreboding is further dramatized by the dark desolate appearance of the mountain ridges behind the wolves and the conflict of colors of the sky above them. A supernatural effect was achieved by twisting the foreground branches into fantastical shapes rather than drawing them like they would more likely appear to be.

Drawn by George S. J. Anderson   1999-2000

Epilog (Endings)

The struggle my wife endured during the time I kept these chronicles is the inspiration that motivated me to finish the stories you have read. I would not feel that I have related the entire story of my struggles with the acceptance and confrontations of my wife's breast cancer unless I explained the remarkable circumstances behind her ordeal.

I feel that this is my watch now, this day, this hour. Twenty-year-old women, thirty-year-old women should not need to live in fear of contracting breast cancer…but they do, and they have! Mammograms, the scientific authorities tell us, do not need to be done on women under the age of forty…but maybe they should be! Everything we knew to be true is now changing by the many challenges of new technology, by envisioning new knowledge, and by realizing that new frontiers are developing from research. Even with all these new prospects on the horizon, we find breast cancer moving down the ranks into a younger age group with deadlier effects. Women must be ever watchful, ever cautious for any sign of this deadly disease.

I am immensely grateful to the physicians, surgeons, and oncologists who have watched with us during our ordeal. I particularly want to thank my wife's surgeon who made such a significant difference in many people's lives with his discovery of breast cancer lurking within her body. As you will realize after reading this story, so much could have been lost if this discovery had not been made. Now, as my final story, (actually a real life history) I would like to relate the remarkable story of my wife's ordeal with breast cancer to you.

"I do not want to be forgotten," she told me a few days after her diagnosis with Stage III breast cancer. Before this diagnosis, she was simply a thirty-nine year old woman going through the daily rituals of running a household, getting to work on time, and making sure our then twelve-year old son got off to school with everything he needed. Breast cancer took the familiar life she knew away from her the day it entered her life.

A few months before this, my wife and son were roughhousing downstairs in our recreation room. I was preparing dinner that summer evening when I heard a sick thud come from the stairwell followed by a penetrating scream. I left the food on the stove and quickly investigated the situation. I discovered my son accidentally kicked her near the top of her right breast. The telltale bruising occurring afterward heralded the presence of a Stage III breast cancer. We later discovered this cancer had been set in motion many years before this fateful injury. The surgeon, who had the dubious duty of having to tell us the site was cancerous, also discovered this particular cancer occurred in only one-tenth of one percent of all breast cancers known to exist. It made it rare and extremely difficult to research. Whatever information we retrieved, we found scattered throughout obscure medical journals or research-oriented medical texts. Since my wife is a Medical Technologist and I am a Registered Nurse, we had better access to this information than most people had. I believe it was here that everything started.

Today's well-known medical advances in the breast cancer arena have improved treatment and therefore more women survive. It is also known that breast cancer incidence is rising. More women are diagnosed than ever before with the disease. Do we believe these increases are caused by improved screening, or improved health education? Even if "yes" is the answer to both, it does not account for increasingly younger women getting breast cancer. You cannot blame an aging population, better screening, or better health education for these increases. We are often blinded by statistics of a "surgical cure" (that is one that extends to five years). The evidence we often don't always hear about are the lifetime "cures." According to the American Cancer Society's 1998 statistics, 67% of women diagnosed with breast cancer survive 10 years, 56% survive 15 years. For a woman diagnosed in her 30's or 40's this is a significant curtailment of life, for a woman diagnosed in her 20's, it is completely unacceptable. My point is, when the subject of breast cancer comes up it is not always taken seriously. I feel disinterest exists because the new advances in the area of breast cancer show the positive end of the story. People often turn a blind eye toward the women whose lives become dramatically changed by breast cancer. Many more lose sight of the women's lives that are lost to this disease.

Today's women are not expected to get a mammogram until they reach the age of forty. When my wife saw her bruise was not healing, she asked her gynecologist for advice. He sent her for a mammogram only weeks before she turned forty. The mammographic results said the tissues were too dense to read. In younger women, this is not an unusual reading. Most times, it is due to the hormonal influences still active in the breast tissues at this age. In my wife's story, it was her first step towards investigating the significance of the non-healing bruise.

By October of 1992, she needed to have a biopsy of the right breast where the bruising was occurring. The bruising, which never seemed to disappear, was caused by an "angiogenic" property, consistent with the type of breast cancer discovered by the biopsy. Angiogenesis meant the tumor was making its own pathways to the blood supply and therefore the bruising. The biopsy also found some of the local lymph nodes contained in the biopsy specimen to be positive as well. This meant not only did cancer exist in her breast, but it had already progressed into her lymph nodes as well. At the time, the significance of this finding was ominous, the emotional effect was traumatic and devastating to us both. During our initial visits with the surgeon and the oncologist, we learned she had a less than forty-percent chance of surviving five years with treatment. Without treatment, she would be dead within two years, possibly less. In November of 1992, she had the mastectomy of the right breast with the hopes that it could possibly save her life.

Through the end of 1992 and most of 1993, she fought a brave and valiant battle. To survive she needed a radical mastectomy but suffered a frozen right shoulder because of it. The condition required six months of physical therapy to restore functioning to the right shoulder, which she fit around her chemotherapy sessions. In addition to all this, she traveled between home and work, a distance of 50 miles each way, and kept her hopes up.

On her first day back at work in December of 1992, her fellow employees gave her a standing ovation when she walked through the door. Little did they know I had driven her to work that day because chemotherapy had weakened her to a point where she could barely stay awake. When I returned later that day, I noticed how much brighter her spirits had become since I left her at work that morning. In my mind, I had expected someone would need to help her walk out the door to the car. Instead, I found her smiling and rushing out to the car to tell me how her first day at work had gone. I could hardly believe it. After she told me the story of the standing ovation she had received upon entering the door to her workplace, I understood what had happened to make her feel this excited. I felt this display of human compassion for one of their own was one very significant spark that ignited her spirit in accomplishing all the things she has done and still plans to do.

By July of 1993, she was informed that her position and others were the casualties of downsizing. My wife learned the true meaning of irony that fateful day when she walked into her workplace of five years and received her layoff notice. Later that same day, her oncologist would inform her that she needed six weeks of radiation. Irony existed when she realized this same job was the one where only months before she had been greeted like a hero. Now, with radiation looming before her, she was wondering how she would pay for it without the insurance her employer provided for her. She also wondered how she would even look for a job with no hair, being too weak to work or look for a job due to the effects of radiation. The telltale radiation marks up the side of her neck were a damning announcement since anyone seeing them would realize she was being treated for cancer. All this was a major setback in her treatment and in her career. It was a change in events for which she could not have prepared, a day that almost crushed her spirit. Eventually some time passed, things worked out with another job, chemotherapy concluded, radiation therapy finally finished, and she was able to go on with her life with some normalcy.

I want to emphasize that the foundations of what my wife was able to accomplish during this period, were proposed and physically started at a time when most of us would be flat on our backs. Very few people would have had the kind of raw courage and stamina it took to achieve the milestones she grasped and held. Her therapies and treatment modalities were a major time commitment themselves. Include in the equation that her job was an hour away from our home and you will realize just how little time she had for herself. Of course, during this time, she was frequently sick from the side effects of chemotherapy and endured many physical therapy treatments to allow normal movements of her right shoulder. Time consuming treatments of chemotherapy and physical therapy continued during the time she investigated the possibility of starting a support group for breast cancer patients and survivors.

As I have mentioned, my wife had problems finding information about her type of breast cancer and its survival rate. One of her foremost desires at the time was to find someone who had been in a similar situation and had survived over a long period. She felt that if someone else like herself could survive for a long time then perhaps she could survive that long as well. At the time, the agencies in our area were not designed to share this kind of in-depth information with her or any other survivors. While the agencies in the area were generous with the information and services they had, the information they offered was often too generalized for her. When she looked into support groups, she found them slanting towards mastectomy patients that incorporated exercise programs into their regimens. The existing breast cancer survivor groups offered emotional support only as a sideline to their exercise programs. Their meeting times were not conducive to working women, and they did not take into account the growing numbers of younger women with breast cancer or the fact that mastectomy was not always the treatment of choice. There were many women walking around devastated by the emotional trauma of a cancer diagnosis that were simply not being dealt with. She found a community not ready to deal with these new women with breast cancer. She wanted to change this.

My wife wanted to create a breast cancer support group which was informative, educational, and most of all, offered emotional support to all breast cancer patients. She wanted a group that would interest people who could speak from authority and experience about the state-of-the-art disciplines involving breast cancer. She wanted this group held at convenient times for working women. My wife, along with the help of several other breast cancer survivors and the York Cancer Center, brought the breast cancer support group known as, "Surviving Breast Cancer," to life in September of 1993, almost a year after her initial diagnosis. Today, the group has over three-hundred members. With the growing success of the group, you can be sure there was a need for this type of group in the community. In 1994, she saw a need for spouses and significant others dealing with breast cancer from another perspective to get together and talk. Now a men's support group meets at the same time as the women's group to discuss their issues.

Allow me to backtrack to a time before the group came into existence to illustrate the kind of heroic efforts my wife made to accomplish all this. Before she went to the Cancer Center with her idea for a support group, she did a lot of research. As she was going through chemotherapy, radiation, physical therapy, and running to and from her full-time job, she researched what a support group needed to get started. She went to seminars on her days off from work when she was feeling good. Between the chemotherapy sessions when she was sick, she watched for every article and piece of information she could find on the subject. She bought books, texts, accessed computer files, and used records from hospital libraries in an effort to educate herself on the subject of breast cancer. She joined NABCO, NBCC, PBCC, and the Y-Me breast cancer support groups to learn what they had to say on the subject. She spoke to other breast cancer survivors outside our area to learn everything she could about starting a group and learned more about her disease in the process. She traveled to any major cities within a three-hour radius that offered seminars on the subject of breast cancer.

She realized although much had been accomplished in the area of breast cancer research, there were political forces at work to hamper funding for additional work. Just before the breast cancer support group had its first meeting, she did something of great importance for herself and the women surviving breast cancer across this nation. In September of 1993, after a vigorous petition drive, in which she took a major part, she made the trip to Washington D. C. to help the thousands of breast cancer survivors deliver petitions to President Clinton. She made the journey just days after finishing radiation therapy and finding a new job. She was still weak from treatments and sported a wig due to her lack of hair growth, but she felt it was so vitally important to be there in that crowd in Washington.

During October of 1993, the breast cancer support group known as Surviving Breast Cancer held its first meeting with about twenty-five women present. This was an overwhelming response to a meeting advertised only by "word of mouth." However, it served to prove the need for a support group like the one she envisioned.

By the early part of 1994, my wife realized that some members were too ill to make it to support group but still wanted some connection with the other survivors. Out of this concern, my wife decided to come up with a support group newsletter. By doing research and using the Internet for information she was able to create a newsletter that was informative, challenging, and kept members up to date on all medical, political, and local happenings. In addition, she created the Network of Survivors, a computer database, which is capable of matching survivors with similar cancer backgrounds.

By this time the local media was beginning to take notice of her work and a Local Cable channel asked her to participate in a TV show with the "Look Good, Feel Better" project sponsored by the American Cancer Society. Two additional Cable TV programs, which highlighted her struggles with breast cancer and advocacy, were produced and aired later that year.

In 1994 she joined the Reach to Recovery program as a volunteer visitor. This program matches breast cancer survivors with newly diagnosed breast cancer patients who have similar circumstances. Lois was diagnosed with a rare type of breast cancer which only appeared in one-tenth of one percent of all breast cancers known to exist. The peculiarity known as an "osteoclast-like giant cell" made the likelihood of finding another woman with the same or similar breast cancer very improbable. Although the idea of finding a "long-time survivor" of this particular breast cancer was something Lois had hoped for, it was not something she would ever accomplish for herself. With the hope of being able to improve this program, since she had not been "well-matched diagnostically" with her visitor, Lois made her mark as a local volunteer and visitor to breast cancer patients. Somehow, in this small way, she realized something for someone else that could not be done for her.

Sometime after the initial breast cancer survivor group started, my wife began getting the same request repeatedly from the women who were attending the sessions. Many of the women wanted to know if someone could talk to their husbands/significant others. Apparently, the breast cancer diagnosis had a significant impact on their spouses and they had concerns about how their spouses/ significant others were dealing with their diagnosis. My wife knew how the experience had affected me, so she requested my help in starting a group for the men. That year the men and significant others were invited to join the breast cancer support group.

In 1995, my wife became involved with the Breast Cancer Awareness Stamp through Diane Sackett Nannery, a woman she met at a conference in Philadelphia. With the help of Ms. Nannery and the help of the Pennsylvania Breast Cancer Coalition (PBCC) she was able to get Pennsylvania involved in a petition campaign for this stamp.

Also during 1995, she was chosen by the Department of Defense to sit on a Scientific Peer Review Panel. These panels are designed to determine funding of scientific research proposals offered to the Department of Defense for breast cancer research and development. She was unable to sit on the panel during this year due to a lack of proposals. Still, it was an honor to have been chosen for such a prestigious role.

By 1996, the first Breast Cancer Awareness Stamp made its way into the post offices across the country. The U.S. Postal Service honored my wife for her help in getting approval for the Breast Cancer Awareness Stamp in Pennsylvania. On June 15, 1996 she coordinated the celebrations for this stamp taking place at three different post offices in York County at the same time. This was quite an accomplishment for a woman who was not sure of her own survival only three and a half years earlier.

At this same time, the Surviving Breast Cancer Support Group has become the largest breast cancer support group in the county with about 150 members participating. During this year, her expertise is recognized by various groups and she is now asked to speak at different functions. Because of her recognition in the area of breast cancer, she had several speaking engagements at local high schools talking to young women about the importance of breast health. She also spoke as a breast cancer survivor to a class of LPN's at York County Vocational-Technical School about breast cancer and treatments. This work continues through today.

In August of this year, she was honored to be chosen to sit on the Department of Defense Peer Review Panel for Breast Cancer Research. She was part of the decision making process to allocate where funds were to be spent for breast cancer research.

Also in 1996, the American Cancer Society initiated a work known as The Skin Deep Exhibit, Stories in the Fight Against Breast Cancer. The patchwork was created by survivors, friends, family, or anyone affected by breast cancer. Each person contributed a ten-inch by ten-inch square with their thoughts, feelings, concepts, ideas, pictures, memories, anything to do with the breast cancer experience and placed it on their square. These squares were then individually glued to a larger backing. Then all the squares were laced together with pink ribbon and presented as a large patchwork. As a volunteer with the American Cancer Society, my wife participated in "The Skin Deep Exhibit, Stories in the Fight Against Breast Cancer," by speaking at a local college and explaining the meaning of the patchwork and her contribution to it. She also participated in a radio show at the local college to promote the "Skin Deep Project." Additionally, as a volunteer for the American Cancer Society, she continues to work with Reach to Recovery.

Later in 1996, she was asked by the Pennsylvania Breast Cancer Coalition to act as a political whip for legislation before the Pennsylvania House of Representatives. This activity involved legislation, which allowed a line at the bottom of the Pennsylvania tax forms for donating money for breast and cervical cancer. The legislation was passed and the line currently appears at the bottom of all the Pennsylvania State Income tax forms.

In 1997, my wife did something which, I feel, was almost superhuman, bigger than life, completely voluntary, and worthy of recognition. The woman who once told me, "I don't want to be forgotten," now put her mark upon the world. In my experiences with cancer, I have seen that it marks itself in a cruel irony but leaves in its wake a legacy of heroes, warriors, and poets. Sometimes you will find that change comes into our lives and makes us different people than the way we were before and sometimes we get the chance to change things. Breast cancer entered my wife's life and changed her. Now her chance to do something about it came to be.

From January 21-23, 1997, the National Cancer Institute (NCI) Director Richard Klausner, MD convened a panel of scientists, which concluded that regular mammograms were not necessary until a woman reached the age of 50. Dr. Klausner disagreed with his own panel as did the American Cancer Society and many other health care agencies. This decision created confusion for the many women approaching the age of 40 as to when to do their first mammogram. The NCI's recommendation, "It is up to the individual and her physician as to when to do the first mammogram," was at odds with the recommendations of other agencies. When all the literature speaks of prevention, when all the insurance companies feel prevention is cheaper that treating an illness, how did the NCI come up with such a statement? A Swedish delegation had been invited to the consensus panel to share new information on this age group. Their evidence showed a 16-25% mortality reduction using screening mammography in 40-49 year old women. Their evidence was the latest available evidence on this age group. They were totally ignored. Some members of the panel were outraged. Jeannie Petrek, MD of Memorial Sloan Kettering Cancer Center in New York City, resigned from the consensus panel because of its decision.

My wife was markedly upset. On a breast cancer discussion list on the Internet, my wife, Lois A. Anderson, and Musa Mayer considered what to do. By January 26th, it was decided they would get as many stories as they could from women under the age of 50 whose breast cancer was discovered by mammograms. Lois decided to take this battle further when she went to the Pennsylvania Breast Cancer Coalition (PBCC). On January 31,1997 Lois and the Pennsylvania Breast Cancer Coalition sent out a news wire calling for stories nationwide to help overturn this decision. On Tuesday February 4, 1997, Senators Specter and Hutchinson were instrumental in passing a non-binding U.S. Senate resolution recommending mammograms to 40-49 year old women across the country. It passed 98 to zero. It did not change the NCI's decision. More needed to be done.

On February 5th, Dr. Richard Klausner, Director of the NCI, spoke before the Subcommittee on Labor, Health, Human Services, Education, and Related Agencies about the "mammogram decision." On the same day, Lois spoke to Dr. Alan Rabson, Deputy Director of the NCI as to what could be done to change the NCI's position on mammograms. In a telephone conversation, they felt that the women who had been helped by the use of a mammogram before the age of 50 might make an important impact. Lois appeared on three local TV stations within the next week calling for stories from women saved by mammograms before the age of 50. The response was overwhelming! Lois manned the telephone during the afternoon and evening and I generally took care of it during the mornings and early afternoon. We both worked at night so the calls kept both of us busy for the next several weeks. On February 14, 1997, Lois "appeared" with Dr. Wanda Filer (then Pennsylvania's State Surgeon General) in a radio broadcast of the Pennsylvania Round Table program. The topic was "Mammograms and the National Cancer Institute's Decision." Between February 1st and February 25th she collected a little over 200 anecdotal stories as evidence to be presented before another NCI meeting on February 25th and 26th. This panel was asked to postpone any decision until later in a move to cool the highly charged atmosphere.

On February 25th, Senator Arlen Specter of Pennsylvania sent a letter inviting Lois to testify before a special hearing of the

Subcommittee on Labor, Health and Human Services, and Education. She continued to gather stories from all over the country by email, faxes, and mail services. On March 3rd, 1997, she walked into the hearings held at Hershey Medical Center with 226 stories from women under the age of 50 whose lives were saved by the use of a mammogram. On the day she went to testify, she told me she was as nervous as the day we were married. I had to tell her that she was going to do well that day and she did. It was a true heroic effort for all women saved by mammograms and all those who have yet to be saved by them in the future. Senator Specter carried all 226 stories and Lois's testimony and made them a part of the Congressional Record.

On March 4th, Senator Specter met with Donna Shalala and put pressure on her to have the NCI change its decision. Can we say Lois was the deciding factor in overturning this decision? I'd say ask Senator Specter….I already know what he will tell you. For the record, we will say Lois greatly affected the way the decision went for the entire country. How many people does that cover? Whatever the population of this country is now I would say. Breast cancer affects us all, not just the women and men who have the disease. Perhaps the world was affected as well since the many nations of the world look to us for leadership in many areas, especially medicine. By making the NCI align their thinking with other health agencies throughout the country it gave women approaching their 40's more guidance as to when to begin having mammograms. I hope that warriors such as Lois will fight again when the need arises.

Poets remember the past and use it to illustrate truths, memories, unsung heroes, and warriors lost in battle. In late September and early October of 1997 Lois was involved in the Pennsylvania Breast Cancer Coalition's "67 Counties, 67 Women," a pictorial overview of women from all the counties of Pennsylvania. She was involved in the Pink Ribbon Walk, which opened the exhibit held at the York Cancer Center at Apple Hill. Later, the York County Commissioners honored her and two other active breast cancer survivors from York County with a proclamation. The exhibit is moving. Many of the women pictured there have died since the photographs were taken some years ago. During this exhibit, two women were remembered who recently passed away before the exhibit was brought to York. These women lost their battles but will be remembered by us all. Lois was a moving force behind the exhibit volunteering many hours to making sure everything went smoothly while it was here. Again, she went before the TV and newspapers spreading her message that there is life beyond breast cancer. She knows that she can aspire to dream of better things, better times, and sometimes life can come out of ashes.

The year 1997 continued to be one of spreading the news about breast cancer when she was nominated and chosen to receive the Jefferson award in the later part of April. She received the award for her volunteerism in the area of breast cancer awareness and her commitment to help all women diagnosed with breast cancer. Later in 1997, she was honored with "The Golden Eagle Award" by a local radio station who also recognized her voluntary efforts in the breast cancer arena.

For the next two years, 1997 and 1998, Lois was chosen to sit on the Department of Defense Peer Review Panel. She has been chosen to sit on a panel by the Healthy Woman 50+ here in Pennsylvania and give her recommendations as well in 1999.

1998 showed the community was behind her when she won the prestigious "Golden Rule Award" sponsored by the J.C. Penny Company for achievement in voluntary works aimed at breast cancer awareness. In 1999, she was nominated as the "Outstanding Woman" in Pennsylvania by the Women of Today. Her experiences create a remarkable story of taking a life threatening illness and turning it into a shining victory for life.

Lois always told me she did not want to be forgotten. When she was diagnosed at the age of thirty-nine she felt she had not yet made her mark upon the world. Breast cancer changed all that for her. Since the day she was diagnosed, she has worked to become a spokesperson and advocate for breast cancer education, information, and emotional support. Breast cancer entered her life and transformed her into a different person than the one she was before. Not just in the obvious physical sense but on a totally different plane of being. She became better, stronger, and potentially more alive than any of us had ever seen her. She truly saw the beauty in the moment and went about living it like it could be the last moment of her life. Like a poet, she has been an inspiration to all that meet her.

How do you explain the time she puts into all of this? Let me put it this way…there is no way I could put it all down in hours, minutes, and seconds. Lois has a way of living and dealing with her breast cancer that makes each day a part of giving of herself to the people who need her advice and help. Lois is both a

Medical Technologist and a breast cancer survivor. She brings the best of both worlds with her and is a force to be reckoned with. As both a survivor and a professional, she has proven her worth for being here.

As of October 12, 1997, Lois became a five-year breast cancer survivor. It seems so easy to write the words five-year survivor but, in fact, the road was fought hard through those times. There have been many setbacks and many close calls. Her vigilance may be the reason we have been graced with her presence these many years later. Still, the reality is that she remains with us and we are all better people for having her here. She was very grateful to have seen her son graduate from high school in 1998. Yet only six years ago, it did not seem to be an entirely realistic goal. Maybe, if all goes well, there may be a good possibility she may even get to see him graduate from college.

So there you have it…there is life after breast cancer. Even with seemingly impossible odds it can be overcome. If you have been touched by breast cancer, you could sit in a corner and hope cancer will not reenter your life, or you can be vigilant and change the world. If you have been fortunate enough not to have been affected by cancer in any form, then use your good fortune and make each day a masterpiece of living. Imagine all that could have been lost if my wife had not survived breast cancer. One person, one idea, a warrior, a poet, and a real life hero…you can really make a difference. So, if you are sitting there thinking about when you'll get started, don't stare out the window in a dream. Dreams are there for the making. Life comes out of ashes. You do get the chance to change things…if you want to.

Finally, this road, this story comes to an end. There is no more paving, no more finished path for us to follow…just the end. Beyond this point is a frontier of discovery, hope, dreams, and new beginnings. At the end of everything, there is a new beginning. This is the end of a beginning. From here, you can go everywhere and anywhere. It is up to you to start.

Flying Kites

We measure our lives by the great events that touch us. Everyday our lives continue in their ordinary ways…ordinary ways that are comforting in their sameness and their predictability. Then comes a great event making all our ordinary days seem like a prelude for something that pulls you closer to heaven, or hell, than anything that has happened before. It is an event so enormous, you know you will never experience anything like it again. Two events in my life were like this…the birth of my son and my wife's diagnosis with breast cancer. All other events flow away from these like silent circles rippling before and behind them.

One strange surreal day, not long ago, my wife was told she had a serious form of breast cancer. In the surgeon's office I listened with her for the word "cure," instead I heard, "disease-free survival." I wanted to hear "ten-years, five-years," or even, "she will be okay for awhile." But as I watched, her surgeon shuddered the ultimate closing to his epistle, "We will hope for five years, after that we don't know…" Inside me, a wounded cry bore into my animal heart, yet I reined it tightly within me. I wanted to take my solitary voice to the dying embers of sky and throw this inner rage like a fiery tempest at the forces that sent this disease to her. However, the heavens were silent, and so was I. We both seemed so insignificantly finite as we looked into the infinite sky. We were afraid to close our eyes…afraid that when they closed we would have to say goodbye forever. We wondered when, and how, and what it would take to be okay again.

Cancer entered my life like a hurricane, knocking down my illusions of what appeared to be valuable like a house of cards. In the aftermath, were the lives around me and a certain will of courage to stand by my wife during her ordeal with breast cancer. At the time, the concepts, predictions, and treatments seemed insurmountable to all of us. Just getting by the enormous hurdle of the word "cancer" was almost more than either of us could bear alone. Despite her poor prognosis, my wife stood against it and survived. In everything she did, in both spirit and demeanor, she wore the mantle of a true warrior fighting this deadly disease. In my eyes and in those who watched with us, she showed us all the stuff of heroes

Now that the hurricane winds of cancer subsided, the winds of what "could be" still remained, reminding us the fight may never be over and might not yet be won. At the end of this hurricane, the winds of change surrounded us, engulfing us in the same force that nearly swept us away. We took small gasps of air and hoped the massive breathing wind did not drown us in its power. We remembered the strength of the wind when it almost took our breath away. It made us feel small and powerless. It was unquestionably more powerful than any man…very few could stand against it. In our fear of its potential effect we could have cowered from it…perhaps we could have hidden from it and never reappeared.

For quite some time, breast cancer made it difficult to consider anything more than what life presented to us each day. As each day faded into the shadows of the past I realized my wife had been spared for some purpose, some reason that seemed nebulous and out of reach. We eventually realized that living in the past, fearing the predictions of short survival, only allowed our remaining time to slowly disappear. We had to learn that the point of survival was not struggling to hold onto life, but that we struggled to live. As the wind passed over us, we had to choose. We could taste the air upon our lips and lose it in a breath upon the moving air, or seize it like a treasure that we locked inside our hearts. This treasure could then become such a part of us that it could change us… could make us different souls than what we were or what we could become.

When my son was still a child, I would take him to the top of the hill behind our house on windy days to fly kites. Standing there together, I would unfurl the colorful mylar, loosen the tether line, and allow the vagabond wind to catch the stretched cloth in its unseen grasp. The kite would sail into that unreachable vastness and float high into the sky, challenging the flight of the birds in the air. Caught in the petulant breezes, it seemed to touch the face of heaven in its flight. When the kite held firm in its course and sailed gracefully in the air, I would hand the tether line to him. His eyes sparkled with delight when he realized he held something that could almost touch the distant clouds. Though the turbulent wind at the top of the hill felt as if it could almost burn our skin in its abrasive grip, there was no reason to fear. What existed was the simple delight of sending a child's colorful sail into the sky like a message sent farther than where our mere hands could reach.

Somehow living with the possibility of cancer returning each day reminded me of the times I flew kites with my son. I thought back upon those days of innocence and realized how we needed to be more like children…unafraid of the wind. On those days when I heard the wind outside my window, it still made my heart race. I had to look inside myself to find the heart of a child. There I found that rage was gone, and hope had taken its place. Abandoning our fears of the wind, we were able to launch our kites into the blustery wind, sending them like messages, using it as a force to get closer to heaven than we could ever reach without it.

Days no longer seem ordinary when you realize the miracle of having those you love around you. Never take for granted those days that seem ordinary and carefree. Days like these may not be that way again, nor may they be as many. Beyond the magic of research, beyond all our mystical science, beyond all our human potential, lies a spirit dreaming of hope. It holds us steadfast in the wind, allowing us to send our prayers upon the wind like children's colorful kites. Our prayers can tell heaven of heroes, warriors, and poets locked in the battle against breast cancer. And, if you ever see kites flying against the vastness of the sky, remember to believe in hope. My wife still sails on beside me seven years later, and my son is about to launch some kites of his own. I look forward to what those kites may bring.

George S. J. Anderson
September 22, 1999

Old Friends

And so Old Friend
The time for our parting
Is at hand
The path we travel
Parts here at this pass
This new road I travel
Has a cause
Much different from yours
So as friends we pass
To be old friends
Parting hands
Finding new ones
To plant in our hearts
Time tolls the bells
Of our keeping
Waking desires
Soft the dreams
While we are sleeping
We have new beginnings
Wrought of flesh and bone
So that we might find new friends
On the tightropes of life
And by chance we may meet again
Old friends
With hopes and desires
While making new friends
Till we make them old friends
As you and I
Must now pass

1978   George S. J. Anderson

ABOUT THE AUTHOR

George S. J. Anderson is the husband of Lois Anderson, a seven-year breast cancer survivor and advocate. He has worked as a registered nurse for twenty-five years and has had many experiences with oncology patients during his career. He facilitates a support group for the husbands/significant others of women with breast cancer for the York Health System in York, Pennsylvania.

He won his first award for poetry in 1974 with a poem entitled *The Cage.* Since that time he has published poems such as *The Hour of the Child, The Fly, Night Visions, Leaves, Old Friends, January,* and *Illusions.* Most recently, he published *Journeys* with the Watermark Press in 2000. In 1994, he self-published the short story *Remember This. Twelve Roses* was published in 1997 in a collection of short stories called *Silver Linings, the Other Side of Cancer.* He does his own artwork for his writings and has been drawing in pencil, charcoal, and pastels since 1982.